"You managed to kill whatever I felt for you."

Greg paused, then shrugged indifferently. "Anyway, it's all in the past, and I suppose I should be grateful for at last learning the truth about why you left me."

Alex said painfully, "If you dislike me now, why did you come on this trip when you knew who you'd be traveling with? You didn't need the money."

"Oddly enough, I rather fancied the job. I love Japan. I...have friends here. You were a complication I could have done without, but I was damned if I was going to turn down the assignment because of it."

He studied her face, watching the understanding slowly surface. Then he said sarcastically, "Finally getting through to you, is it?"

KAY THORPE, an English author, has always been able to spin a good yarn. In fact, her teachers said she was the best storyteller in the school—particularly with excuses for being late! Kay then explored a few unsatisfactory career paths before giving rein to her imagination and hitting the jackpot with her first romance novel. After a roundabout route, she'd found her niche at last. The author is married with one son.

Books by Kay Thorpe

HARLEQUIN PRESENTS
822—DOUBLE DECEPTION
853—SOUTH SEAS AFFAIR
902—DANGEROUS MOONLIGHT
941—WIN OR LOSE
973—JUNGLE ISLAND
1084—TIME OUT OF MIND
1141—LAND OF ILLUSION

HARLEQUIN ROMANCE
2151—TIMBER BOSS
2232—THE WILDERNESS TRAIL
2234—FULL CIRCLE

Don't miss any of our special offers. Write to us at the following address for information on our newest releases.

Harlequin Reader Service
901 Fuhrmann Blvd., P.O. Box 1397, Buffalo, NY 14240
Canadian address: P.O. Box 603,
Fort Erie, Ont. L2A 5X3

KAY THORPE

tokyo tryst

Harlequin Books

TORONTO • NEW YORK • LONDON
AMSTERDAM • PARIS • SYDNEY • HAMBURG
STOCKHOLM • ATHENS • TOKYO • MILAN

Harlequin Presents first edition September 1989
ISBN 0-373-11204-1

Original hardcover edition published in 1988
by Mills & Boon Limited

CHAPTER ONE

'THE Chief wants to see you, Miss Darwin,' announced the newest and youngest member of the staff cheerfully, popping his head round the partition. 'He said to go right on in.'

Alex put down the bottle of Tipp-Ex with a sigh, running a hand beneath the heavy fall of pale red-gold hair to ease the back of her neck. 'Did he say what it was about?'

The question came too late; the owner of the head had already moved on. Not that it was likely he would have been able to supply an answer, in any case, Alex conceded, pushing back her chair to get to her feet. With any luck, Ben had a new assignment for her. Anything had to be better than the piece she was working on right now.

Partitioned into separate offices, the floor was a hive of activity, mostly due to the close proximity of the monthly publication date. Putting together a magazine of the quality and scope of *World* was no simple affair. No matter how far ahead the layout was planned, there were always the last-minute additions or alterations— space to be made, space to be filled. Panic was a way of life for the third week in each month. Alex often thought she would feel lost without it.

The editor's office was one of the few totally enclosed. One day, Alex promised herself philosophically, she would aspire to such heights. He was speaking on the telephone when she entered the room, and waved her to a seat without interrupting his flow, greying beard bristling with fury. 'I don't care how you get it, just get it!' he concluded, slamming the receiver back on to its rest with a thud that should have snapped the instrument in two.

'More problems?' asked Alex on a note of sympathy.

'Nothing that can't be sorted, given a little co-operation.' Quick to flare and equally quick to fade, he was already in command of himself again. In his early fifties, he had the weatherbeaten features and far-seeing eyes of the outdoor man: an impression enhanced by the growth of hair covering the lower half of his face. Not editor material at all as she knew it, had been Alex's impression on first meeting him six months ago. She knew better now, of course. Ben Reynolds was not just a good editor-in-chief, he was one of the best.

'What can I do for you?' he tagged on.

'*You* wanted to see *me*,' she said, and saw his expression clear.

'That's right, I did.' He studied her a moment, taking in the clean oval of her face, the widely spaced green eyes and softly curved mouth. 'What do you know about Japan?'

Alex felt her heart give a jerk of anticipation. 'Not too much,' she acknowledged. 'Why?'

'We're planning on running a special feature in the December issue,' he said. 'I want contrasts—the real Japan as opposed to the one the tourists see. Can do?'

Her eyes were sparkling. 'When do I leave?'

'Not so fast.' Ben was smiling, too, well aware of the opportunity on offer. 'It's going to be stinking hot out there in August, you realise?'

'Who cares about a little heat?' came the ready rejoinder. 'I'll buy myself a parasol when I get there. As I said, how soon do I go?'

He grinned. 'That's what I like to see—eagerness! Monday OK?'

Three days, she thought. Long enough if she worked at it. 'Fine,' she said. 'Who's going to be coming with me? Danny?'

Ben shook his head. 'We're not using a staff photographer. You're going to need somebody with a feel for the kind of world you're going to be writing about. Somebody who's travelled extensively in Japan and knows all the rules of conduct. Very important to the Japanese, apparently. You've heard of Greg Wilde, I imagine?'

Alex didn't move a muscle. Her face felt suddenly frozen. When she spoke, her voice sounded thick. 'I've heard of him.'

'Well, he's agreed to do it. What's more, he can set up just the kind of inside look we're aiming for. He's been a regular visitor to Japan for many years. Even speaks the language.' He was looking at her oddly. 'Something wrong?'

She made an effort to smile, to recover her poise. 'Does he know who's going to be doing the write-up?'

'He knows it's a woman, if that's what's bothering you.' There was an ironic note in his voice. 'So far as I'm aware, he doesn't have anything against women.'

Too true, thought Alex with an irony of her own. It wasn't what she had meant, but she didn't bother to correct the impression. 'How come I got the job?' she asked instead. 'Tony Jackman usually has the pick off the tree.'

'It was a toss-up between the two of you.' There was surprise now in the editor's voice. 'You having second thoughts?' he demanded bluntly.

It was impossible, Alex reflected, to explain her feelings at this moment. Greg Wilde. Of all the people in the world, it had to be Greg! It was almost two years since she had last seen him. Not long enough to forget the pain he had caused her—nor to forgive the hurt. To have him as her travelling companion on this trip would be unpalatable, to say the least, yet if she backed out now it was unlikely if another chance like this would be coming her way for a long time—if ever. Ben was paying her the greatest of compliments in selecting her ahead of Tony Jackman, who was a fine writer himself. Turning it down would be like slapping him in the face. He would hardly take kindly to that.

'No, of course not,' she said, giving herself no time to make that mistake. 'Just trying to be sympathetic to the loser, that's all.'

'Big of you.' From his dryness of tone, Ben was not wholly deceived. 'I'm sure he'd feel the same way.' He straightened in his chair as a knock came on the door. 'This should be Wilde now.'

Alex made no move as the door opened in answer to the shouted invitation. Ben's secretary announced the visitor's name and ushered him in, closing the door again as she departed. Ben came round the desk to greet the newcomer with hand outstretched.

'Glad you could make it. I thought it would be a good idea if we got together over a few details.'

'Sounds reasonable.' The deep-timbred voice sent a tremor of memory down Alex's spine. 'I've already been in touch with some people out there. No problems so far.'

'Good.' There was a pause: Alex could feel Ben's eyes on her back. She forced herself to turn her head as he added, 'Meet your co-traveller,' looking up into the vivid blue eyes with the same tautening of stomach muscle his glance had always elicited in the past.

'Mr. Wilde.' She nodded coolly. 'Nice to meet you.'

If there had been any shock at all, he wasn't revealing it. He took the cue smoothly. 'Same goes. It should be quite a trip.'

'Two weeks should cover it,' said Ben, getting straight down to business as the younger man took the other chair on Alex's side of the desk. 'Your tickets out are ready-booked. Where you go when you get there depends largely on what you come up with. There'll be an expense account to draw on, naturally, though I'd be grateful if you can keep it within reasonable limits.'

'Will do.' The younger man sounded businesslike himself. 'You realise we'll only be scratching the surface in two weeks?'

'It's going to be up to Alex here to give it some depth,' came the prompt response.

The dark head turned her way, one eyebrow lifting with faint irony. 'Good at it, are you?'

'She wouldn't be going if she weren't.' A faint line appeared between Ben's brows as he looked from one to the other. 'You two met before?' he asked on a doubtful note.

'Not at all,' said Alex swiftly. 'And yes, I am good at it, Mr Wilde. The same way you're good at what you do. I'm just a little surprised that your commitments allow you to take two weeks out at short notice, that's all.'

'Let's just say it was too good an opportunity to turn down,' he responded. 'It's over a year since I was last in Japan. This way I can kill two birds with one stone.'

The sudden spark in the blue eyes made the words sound almost like a threat. Alex withdrew her gaze, looking down at the hands clasped about her lifted knee, seeing the whitened knuckles. He hadn't changed one iota: the same lean, hard-boned features, mouth slightly tilted at one corner in the manner she knew so well, thick dark hair showing no hint of grey as yet. Clad in casual trousers and jacket, he looked just as fit as he always had. But then, at thirty-four, he was still in his prime.

'What did you have in mind?' she asked.

'A couple of days in Tokyo for starters,' he said. 'There's plenty there that the average tourist wouldn't know about. Then I've friends in Kyoto who will give you some insight into how a traditional Japanese home is run. After that, Shikoku Island for a look at the old Japan before industry took over.'

Alex made herself look directly at nim again. 'It doesn't sound a great deal to fill in two weeks.'

'Believe me,' he said, 'you'll find plenty to write about. I'll make sure of it.'

That glint again. Alex steeled herself against the sudden trepidation. He wasn't going to rob her of this chance. Not under any circumstances. She might be the one who had ended their relationship two years ago, but he was the one who had instigated that finish. There had been no accusations then and there wouldn't be now, whatever he said to her. Let him go on believing that *she* had grown tired of *him*! At least her pride stayed intact.

'What about accommodation in Tokyo?' asked Ben. 'Do we book you into a hotel?'

'You'd probably have difficulty this time of year,' Greg replied. 'Apart from the tourists, the Japanese take their main holidays in August. Leave it with me. I have contacts who'll get us into a *ryoken*. That's a Japanese-style hotel as opposed to the Westernised,' he added. 'If we're going to see the real country it has to be wholesale.'

'I'll make sure to pack my kimono,' declared Alex drily, receiving a bland smile in return.

'There's more to being Japanese than putting on the costume, as you're going to discover. Even allowing for Western influences, it's another world out there.'

'With the women still very much second-class citizens, from what we hear!'

The smile came again, infuriating in its mockery. 'I shouldn't have thought pre-judgement an asset in your line of work.'

Alex bit her lip, aware of Ben's mounting irritation. He didn't understand the situation, of course. Even if he had known of their prior association, he couldn't be expected to understand her reactions. To a man of Ben Reynolds' ilk, the job came before any other consideration. It was a view worth cultivating—especially now.

'I'll do my best to keep an open mind,' she said. 'What time is the flight on Monday?'

'Eleven-thirty,' Ben acknowledged. 'With a nine-hour time jump, it's going to be Tuesday when you land.'

'Eight-hour,' Greg corrected. 'Allowing for British Summertime, that is.'

Pedant, thought Alex, making a mental note of that small fact none the less. Not for the first time she wished she were as proficient a photographer as she was a writer, in which case this situation need never have arisen. Except that she still wouldn't have been able to speak the language, prompted the voice of reason, and for what she wanted to do that was going to be an essential requirement.

The strident summons of the telephone interrupted Ben's next remark. He made a sound of impatience under his breath as he snatched it up. 'Yes?' he barked.

The one-sided altercation that followed was so much a part of the general texture of pre-publication week that Alex could turn her mind off from it and think her own thoughts. Not that she was going to come to any far-seeing conclusions, she admitted wryly. Like it or not, she was stuck with the arrangement as it stood. How Greg himself was feeling about it was difficult to guess. In all probability she had been reading too much into too little when it came to reactions. There was a precedent there, wasn't there? From that very first meeting...

She had been aware for some time of the man behind the camera on the far side of the raised catwalk, especially as he himself kept glancing her way in between shots. She knew who he was, of course. Greg Wilde was already an established name in the world of photography. Not just fashion, either. He covered the whole spectrum. Just a few months ago he had brought out a book of off-the-beaten-track studies that had done extremely well in the non-fiction lists.

He was rather devastating himself, she reflected, the dark hair glinting with health and vitality where it caught the light, features so definitively masculine in their chiselled lines. No more than the early thirties, for sure, which made his success doubly admirable.

The show reached its well-orchestrated conclusion, drawing deserved applause from the audience. Not one of the top collections, but certainly a designer to be reckoned with next season, if she was any judge at all. The magazine might do well to run a feature on him during the coming months. His clothes held street appeal.

People were rising to their feet, beginning to drift away. Alex put away her notebook in the capacious handbag-cum-briefcase she always carried and followed suit. The exit doors were over the far side of the room beyond the catwalk. Rounding the end of the latter, she found her immediate passage blocked by the man packing away equipment. Whether by accident or design she couldn't be sure, but there was nothing apologetic about the blue gaze turned on her as she paused.

'This won't take a minute,' he promised. 'Would you might just holding that for me,' handing her a lens, 'while I find the cap?'

Alex accepted the delay with good grace. Not much point in going back to the office anyway, when it was already gone five. She studied the back of the dark head as Greg Wilde bent over his camera case, liking the clean-cut line of his hair falling short of his shirt collar. Not the arty type at all, despite the pale suede jacket. Broad shoulders, she noted in passing, and lean hips. Upright, he must be all of six feet tall.

Her reckoning was faulty, she realised a little bemusedly when he straightened with the missing lens cap triumphantly in his grasp. In her three-inch heels, she still came no higher than his jawline. A strong jaw too, the mouth firm and well-shaped. Alex registered the faint tensing of muscle down in the pit of her stomach without particular surprise. Few women with normal reflexes could fail to be aware of his masculine appeal, and her reflexes were very normal indeed.

'Got it!' he exclaimed. He took the lens from her, smiling into her eyes. 'Thanks. You're with *Parade*, aren't you?'

'Yes,' she acknowledged, taken aback. 'How did you know that?'

The smile acquired an extra tilt. 'I asked.'

Gaze direct, she said, 'Why?'

He laughed. 'I'd have thought that pretty obvious. You knew I was watching you.'

It was Alex's turn to smile. 'My attention was on the show. It's what I was here for.'

'Me too. Only I kept catching you in the viewfinder.' The blue eyes held a dancing light. 'The problem with using a wide-angle lens. I thought we might have dinner together.'

Alex wasn't often stuck for words, but the invitation somehow left her floundering a little. 'I don't think I . . .'

'The name's Greg Wilde,' he interrupted smoothly. 'I'm unattached, solvent and fairly respectable. If it's an independent character-reference I need, maybe . . .'

She was laughing herself now, shaking her head in negation. 'I don't think that's going to be necessary. Your name speaks for itself.'

'That's a relief.' One dark brow lifted quizzically. 'So?'

'It's too early for dinner,' she prevaricated, not at all sure why she was being so evasive. 'And too late for tea.'

'So we'll have a couple of drinks somewhere first. Gives us chance to talk.'

'About what?' she challenged.

'Us,' came the ready reply. 'I've got the car a couple of streets away. I'll bring it round the front while you stand by my equipment. That way I'll be sure you'll still be here when I get back.'

Faced with a straight choice, Alex gave in to the dictates of her senses. It wasn't as if she had anything else on for this evening. Greg Wilde both attracted and intrigued her. Suffering from no false modesty about her own looks, she none the less wouldn't have counted herself as the type to draw attention from a man as accustomed to female beauty as he must be. True, her hair had always been a focus of interest because the true Titian was comparatively rare, which fact might well have caught his professional eye initially. Whatever his reasons for asking her out, she was going anyway. What did she have to lose?

She waited on the pavement outside the hall while he went to fetch the car, the camera case at her feet. The early evening traffic was dense. It took him almost fifteen minutes to get back alongside with the dark blue Jaguar.

'Sorry about that,' he said, coming to lift the case into the boot before stowing her equally safely into the front passenger seat. 'At this time of day nobody gives way. Fasten your belt, will you?'

Alex pulled down the visor flap as he went round to slide behind the wheel, checking her make-up in the mirror with a judicious eye. She was wearing a bold black and ecru striped jacket over a plain black dress, her shoulder-length hair held off her face by a narrower-striped bandeau in the same colours. Long hair was on its way back, according to the pundits. So far as she was concerned, it had never been out. She had the ends trimmed and shaped every three months at a good salon, and washed it herself whenever she felt the need. The cost of city-living stretched her salary far enough without paying through the nose for a shampoo and set.

'You'll do,' commented Greg lightly, forcing his way back into the traffic stream by sheer nerve. 'Very well, in fact. You won't mind if we make a detour to drop off my equipment before going in search of that drink? The car can be replaced without too much heartache if it gets stolen, other things can't.'

He was apparently taking her agreement as said. Alex couldn't find it in herself to raise objections. 'Wouldn't you find it simpler to use taxis?' she murmured. 'Most other people do.'

'I'm not most other people,' came the equable reply.

That was true enough, she reflected. Greg Wilde was as individual as they came. She stole a glance at the firm profile, pulses quickening to the impact. Not the first man to affect her physically this way, but one with whom she felt an unprecedented sense of rightness. She had a feeling that tonight might be the start of something particularly good.

She had anticipated a call at the studio, but instead he drove out to West Kensington where he had a flat.

'I thought I might snatch a shower and shave, and a change of clothes,' he said unabashedly outside the big old converted house. 'I've been on the go since ten this morning.' Blue eyes assessed her reaction with a glint of humour. 'Not a ruse to get you into a compromising situation. You can sit down here in the car and wait, if you'd rather.'

'I could have met you later, if it comes to that,' Alex pointed out, and saw the humour increase.

'But that wouldn't have given me nearly as much of your company. Anyway, I know a place near here where the food is superb.' He quirked an eyebrow. 'So are you coming up or aren't you?'

Her shrug was light. 'Why not?'

The house contained three flats in all. Greg's lay on the first floor. Showing her into the large and comfortable living-room, he invited her to make herself at home and vanished in the direction of what Alex took to be his bedroom. She could hear him whistling, then the sound of running water. Fifteen minutes, he had said. Time to relax and appraise her surroundings.

There were books on the shelves either side of the mahogany fireplace, many of them, understandably, on photography. The fiction appeared to be an eclectic mixture catering to a wide and free-ranging taste, and told her little about the inner man. Several black and white prints in varying sizes were hung on the walls, one or two framed, the rest left to make their own statement. Knowing even as little as she did about the art of photography, Alex could recognise the quality of these examples. Whatever else, Greg Wilde was on top of his chosen profession.

She was sitting on one of the two-seater sofas glancing through a book of slides when he returned to the room. He had changed into a dark blue suit with a pale pink shirt and navy tie, his jawline smooth and unshadowed. Towelled and brushed, his hair still retained a hint of moisture, curling a little at the ends. A man difficult to resist, came the thought, hastily shunted to the back of her mind where it could do least harm.

'How about a drink here before we leave?' he suggested. 'I've a fairly good selection in.'

'I don't mind,' she said. 'Gin and tonic for me, please.'

'Ice and lemon?'

'If you have it.' Catching his glance, she laughed. 'I know, you'd hardly be offering if you didn't! Just one of those ridiculous things you say without thinking about it.'

'Not nervous of me, are you?' he queried lightly as he moved across to open an inlaid cabinet and extract bottles and glasses. 'I'm relatively harmless.'

'Relative to what?' she responded, entering into the same spirit.

'That,' he said, 'is for you to decide on closer acquaintance.'

She said softly, 'One swallow doth not a summer make.'

'It's a start.' There was glint of gold at one tanned wrist as he poured the tonic. 'The ice is in the fridge. I won't take a moment.'

Alex watched him go from the room, aware of his male magnetism. She would have been the first to scoff at the very notion of love at first sight, yet she had to admit that he already exerted an undue influence on her. She wanted to know more about him—to get inside that dark head of his and discover the real Greg Wilde.

He poured himself a double whisky after supplying her needs, holding the glass out to her with a hint of a smile. 'We'll take a taxi from here,' he said. 'Otherwise you'll have to drink a bottle of wine to yourself!' He paused, eyes lingering a moment on the fullness of her mouth, the smile slowly changing character. 'To friendship,' he offered. 'Old, and new.'

* * *

They saw each other every night for a week. For Alex it was a week of sheer heaven as she cast discretion aside for once and allowed emotion to take over her life. Greg was everything she had ever hoped to find in a man, and more. If there were depths in him she found difficult to reach, she closed both heart and mind to it.

She knew all she needed to know, she told herself when she thought about it at all: his background, his ambitions, his interests. He had spent the greater part of his youth in Japan, where his family had been domiciled through business. It was there that he had first developed his fascination with photography. He was thirty-two years of age to her twenty-three, and possessed of the kind of self-confidence younger men had still to acquire. They shared a like sense of humour, the same tastes in music, a love of the theatre and a scorn of all things pretentious. What more could anyone want than that?

The night they made love for the first time was the culmination of Alex's dreams. They had been to a concert at the Barbican, returning to the flat for a late supper prepared, as Greg himself put it, by his own hands.

'You know, you've never once mentioned your family,' he said over coffee. 'Do you see much of them?'

They had lit the glowing 'coal' gas fire because the evening had turned cool. Alex was watching the licking flames. 'They're dead,' she said levelly. 'Motorway accident when I was three. I survived, they didn't.'

'I'm sorry.' His tone was gentle. 'So who brought you up?'

'My grandparents, only they're gone too, now.' She lifted steady green eyes. 'I barely remember my mother and father, so don't feel too sad for me. I had a happy enough childhood.'

The smile came slow and warm. 'I'm sure you did. Otherwise you wouldn't be as well balanced as you are.'

She laughed. 'Is that how you see me?'

'Most of the time.'

'And the rest?'

Blue eyes took on a glow that had nothing to do with the firelight. 'There are moments when I feel pretty positive that you feel the same way about me as I do about you. Tell me if I'm wrong.'

She drew in a suddenly unsteady breath. 'That would depend,' she got out, 'on what it is you *do* feel.'

He put down the coffee-cup and reached for her, cupping her face between his two hands to kiss her on the lips, not hard, not demanding, but with a tenderness that brought a lump to her throat.

'I love you,' he said. 'I want to make love to you. I think I've wanted it since the very first moment I saw you sitting there on the other side of that catwalk. You're different.'

'From what?' she whispered.

'Just different.' He smoothed back the hair from her temples, studying her features with an intensity that made her heart beat faster. 'Some time I'm going to get around to photographing you, only right now that's not the most pressing need in my life.' He waited, mouth slanting when she failed to respond. 'Say *some*thing, even if it's only goodbye!'

She said huskily, 'Is it really possible to fall in love with someone in a week?'

'It is if it happens.'

He brought down a hand to touch a fingertip to her mouth, lightly tracing the line. This time when he kissed her her lips were ready parted, quivering a little as he sought the inner softness. There was no doubt in her heart that she wanted this. The need had been building in her all evening.

It took bare moments to shed their clothing, both of them too fired to wait. His skin was smooth beneath her questing hands, dark against the creamy whiteness of her own. The subtle scent of his aftershave tantalised her nostrils, a spur to senses already aroused. When he dropped his head to find her breast she arched beneath him, the moan torn from deep within her throat, her fingers turned to claws that clutched and held as if they would never let go.

He was passionate in his possession, but not brutal. Feeling him inside her was the most wonderful sensation in her life to date. She followed where he led, the two of them washed by firelight as they crested the wave to fall into the mindless depths of utter fulfilment.

'Stay with me tonight,' he murmured softly in her ear some untold time later. 'Better still—move in with me.'

Alex lay still in his arms, hardly daring to breathe. 'You don't know what you're saying,' she whispered.

'I was never more aware of it,' he said. He lifted his head to look down at her, eyes piercing her defences. 'We're good for each other, Alex.'

She wanted him to say again that he loved her, but he didn't. Not then. Not that it made any real difference, because she could no more say no to him now than fly.

'When?' she asked, and saw his face relax.

'What's wrong with tomorrow?'

* * *

In actual fact, it took another week to complete the move. A week during which Alex turned a blind eye and a deaf ear to any doubts. Marriage had not been, and perhaps never would be, mentioned, but it wasn't a state to which she herself particularly aspired at this point in her life. What she wanted was to be with Greg. It was as simple as that. She looked no further ahead than each day as it came.

Those first couple of months were idyllic. They had their moments of disagreement, of course, and on one memorable occasion a near fight. Par for any course, Greg called it, when they'd made it up again. Total harmony could only be dull.

The change in him was so gradual, Alex scarcely noted it initially. His work took him quite often out of town, but then so did hers. It was only after she met Samantha Price that she began suspecting the truth, and by then it was already too late.

Samantha was a model, at present under contract to one of the cosmetic companies for which Greg did work. Blonde and beautiful was a trite description, but it fitted her like a glove. The party that evening was to celebrate the launch of a new line, with Samantha very much to the forefront as the face which, it was hoped, would persuade a few million women the world over to buy the products.

'I have Greg to thank for getting me this job,' she claimed when Alex congratulated her. 'The portfolio he did for me was what really swung the deal.' Tawny eyes swung to the man in question standing at Alex's side, the look of intimacy unmistakable—to Alex, at least. 'I'll always be grateful.'

Greg laughed. 'I'll remind you of that if I ever lose my touch and find myself on my uppers!'

'Not much chance of that,' she sparkled back, 'but I'll put by the odd crust just in case!'

'You did a whole portfolio for her?' queried Alex as they moved away from the group surrounding the star of the evening. 'That must have cost her a packet!'

'Not a penny,' Greg returned easily. 'Her face is a photographer's dream. The nearest to Garbo's bone structure I've seen. The shots I put together for her were a small enough return.' He glanced her way when she failed to make any comment, a faint line drawn between his brows. 'She's not nearly as confident as she comes across. If this job proves a failure she'll have a hard time getting back up.'

'I'll take your word for it,' said Alex on the same inconsequential note she had used before. 'Shall we go and get something to eat? I'm starving!'

'You find a seat and I'll fetch a couple of plates over,' he said on a suddenly brittle note. 'We must keep up your strength!'

Biting her lip, Alex watched him move away through the throng. His moods had been unpredictable for some time now, she thought, although it hadn't really come home to her so much until this moment. It had been more than three weeks since he had last told her he loved her, she realised. In so many words, at any rate. Her own fault—or some other outside influence? The constriction in her throat was not to be swallowed.

It was all downhill from there, not least because she found it difficult to put up any real pretence of normality. Samantha's name was never mentioned, but she was right there between them like some beautiful ghost.

She suspected Greg was seeing her yet shrank from attempting to gather proof. What hold did she have on him when all was said and done? His live-in lover, that was her role.

The trip to Paris would at one time have sent her into transports of delight. Under the circumstances she took little pleasure in preparing for it. Greg accepted her departure without apparent regret, although he did accompany her to the airport.

'If you let me know which flight you'll be coming back on, I'll try to make it out to pick you up,' he said at Passport Control. The eyes searching her features held an odd expression, as if they were looking for something no longer there. Yet when he kissed her it was almost the old Greg again, drawing response from her despite herself. 'Take care,' he said softly. 'There are things we have to talk about when you get back.'

She wanted to ask him then what kind of things, but they were already calling her flight. Her last glimpse of him was as he turned and strode away across the concourse, drawing eyes in his lean, lithe passage.

It was three full days before she could bring herself to contact him. Three hectic days in which there had been little time to brood. She timed the call for seven-thirty in the evening London time, reckoning that was the best chance of catching him should he be planning an evening out. The long-delayed lifting of the receiver forestalled her move to replace her own instrument by a bare second.

'Hello?' said a female, instantly recognisable voice. 'This is Greg Wilde's flat.'

Alex put out a slow hand and depressed the rest, sitting there on the mattress-edge with the heaviness seeping through her whole body. So that was that. There could only be one reason for Samantha Price to be at the flat at this time. Greg would no doubt be in the shower preparing to take his new love out on the town. And afterwards? She couldn't bear it, she thought numbly. Not now the evidence was staring her in the face.

Yet what did she have when it all boiled down? came the small voice of reason some immeasurable time later. Samantha might be there at the flat, but she had no proof that they planned to spend the night together. The benefit of the doubt, that was what she had to give him. Innocent until proven guilty.

She rang again the following evening, steeling herself for the sound of Samantha's voice. Greg's deep-timbred tones brought a temporary relief, soon dispelled by the lack of warmth in his greeting. He had tried twice to reach her earlier in the week, he said. Hadn't she got his messages? Alex hadn't, and said so, but there remained some doubt as to whether she was fully believed.

'I've an out-of-town job tomorrow,' he tagged on almost casually towards the end of the somewhat stilted exchange of news—during which he made no mention at all of Samantha's visit. 'I'll be away overnight, so there's a chance I might not make it to the airport in time to meet your flight.'

'No problem,' Alex responded coolly. 'I can handle it.'

There was irony in his reply. 'For sure. See you in forty-eight hours or so, then.'

She sat for some time thinking about it before finally making up her mind. Her job here was just about done. A day wasn't going to make much difference. Returning home early was a futile gesture, she supposed, yet she

couldn't bear the thought of another whole day trying
to show interest in something as unimportant to her at
the moment as fashion. She wanted to be there when
Greg arrived, to thrash out this whole situation and get
at the truth. What she would do if her suspicions proved
to be correct was yet to be decided. Right now she could
only cling to the slim hope that she was mistaken all
along the line.

Her arrival back at the flat around three coincided
with the departure of Mrs Purvey, the twice weekly domestic help.

'Couldn't make it this morning,' proffered the latter,
'due to my hubby being taken bad and I'd to wait in for
the doctor coming.'

'I hope it isn't serious,' said Alex, and received a shake
of the head.

'Nothing a couple of days in bed won't cure. I've given
the bedroom and kitchen a good turn-out. I'll tackle the
living-room Monday.'

Without Greg there to greet her, the flat felt cold and
empty. At one time there would have been a note waiting
for her in like circumstances; today there was nothing.
Disconsolately, she took her suitcase through to the
bedroom to unpack, sorting out things to be laundered
and stowing the rest back into drawers and wardrobe
before turning to her vanity case. The top of the dressing-
table had been swept clear of everything bar the fragile
crystal jar that was Alex's own, passed down from her
grandmother. When Mrs Purvey cleaned, she did it
thoroughly.

Opening the left-hand drawer, Alex smiled involuntarily to see her make-up tray so neat and tidy—a smile
that rapidly faded as her eyes fell on the small, em-

broidered pouch lying next to it. A handbag tissue-holder, that was obvious, only it wasn't hers.

Stretching out a slow hand, she turned the pouch over, scarcely needing the interwoven initial 'S' to consolidate suspicion into fact. Samantha had been right here in the bedroom, seated at this mirror while she repaired the wear and tear of Greg's lovemaking—perhaps even starting from scratch having spent the whole night.

There was no pain at first, just a dreadful numbness. The anger grew from deep down, curling sharp tendrils into every part of her body. She gave herself no time to think, to consider her actions, flinging open the wardrobe doors to yank hangers down from the rail, emptying drawers and piling everything she could manage to get into two suitcases. Whatever was left she would collect tomorrow before Greg returned. For now, all she wanted was to be out of this place—out of his life. Let Samantha have him!

She went to a hotel, where she spent a sleepless, dry-eyed night considering a future totally and utterly bleak. It was her own fault, of course, for putting her trust in a man she scarcely knew, only that was no mitigation for what he had done. The desire for revenge was born in the small hours, developing with every painful beat of her heart to a point where it filled her mind to the exclusion of everything else. Hell hath no fury indeed! she thought. She would show him!

Morning brought no change of heart. If anything, the so-called cold light of day only served to firm her resolve. She was at the flat by ten, and away again before the half-hour, the brief letter she left for him a face-saver in every way.

She wouldn't be coming back, she had said, because for her the affair was over—dead—the whole thing a bore she could no longer endure. Her key she left on the hall table beside the envelope—a gesture of finality that cut right down to the bone. It was done with. Now she had to pick up the pieces and put the whole episode behind her.

Which was easier said than done. She was on her own in the office she shared with two others when Greg came to find her that same afternoon. Looking up to see him standing in the doorway brought her heart into her throat.

'Now *say* it to me,' he said.

'There's nothing left to say,' Alex denied, taking a grip on her emotions. 'I'm sorry if the letter appeared callous. It just seemed the best way at the time.'

His laugh was singularly lacking in humour. 'Callous is hardly the word. Try cowardice for size!' He came into the room, closing the door to stand with his back against it and a look of steel in his eyes. 'Who's the new love in your life?'

Face as cold and controlled as his, she said levelly, 'There is no new love in my life. If you want the truth, I don't happen to think the game is worth the effort!'

His mouth curled. 'What's that supposed to mean?'

'It should be simple enough for someone of your intellect to work out,' she retorted, filled with the need to hurt him the way she had been hurt. 'You might consider yourself one of the world's great lovers, Greg, but so far as I'm concerned, the performance soon palled. If there's any cowardice involved at all it's in not leaving earlier. Paris decided me. The men over there know how to treat a woman!'

'Do they?' He said it softly, so softly, a hint of cruelty
in the curl of his lip. 'Then let's have an up-to-date comparison, shall we?'

He was across at the desk before she could move,
dragging her to her feet. His mouth was hard, demanding, totally without mercy, his hands roving her
body with a roughness as hurtful in its intent as its
physical contact. She was too stunned to struggle against
him. All she could think was that this couldn't really be
happening; that the whole thing was some dreadful
nightmare. When he suddenly thrust her from him she
was so unbalanced she almost fell.

'You're not worth the trouble,' he gritted. 'Go on back
to your Frenchmen!'

CHAPTER TWO

THE slam of the door echoed again in Alex's mind, bringing her back to the present with a start to find Ben regarding her with interrogatively raised brows, his hand still resting on the receiver he had just replaced.

'You still with us?' he enquired.

'I'm sorry,' she said, giving herself a mental shake, 'I was thinking about what I've to do before we leave. Did you say something?'

'I suggested you and Greg took yourselves off together to finalise arrangements over a drink,' he repeated. 'It's nearly five, anyway, and I'm going to be tied up for the next hour or so.'

'It's too early for a drink,' Alex stalled, and sensed derision in the man seated next to her.

'It doesn't have to be alcoholic. There's a coffee-bar down the road.' He was getting to his feet as he spoke, a latent power in the way he moved. 'Shall we go?'

With Ben there she had no alternative but to agree, although arrangements, she thought, could easily have been made over the phone. They were flying to Japan on Monday at eleven-thirty. If it came to that, what other details were necessary? Once they got to their destination she was in his hands, anyway—a thought which brought a sudden quiver of apprehension.

Despise him she might, she told herself stoutly; afraid of him she refused to be. Whatever the blow to his male pride two years ago, he was over it now. They could never be friends, of course, but they could perhaps form an adequate working relationship for the coming two weeks. Outside of the job itself, they need have little to do with each other.

The coffee-bar was crowded, the only seats available right at the back where a long shelf had been erected as a resting place for cups and plates. Greg went to fetch two coffees while Alex saved the seats, returning with a large slab of chocolate cake for himself in addition.

'I didn't get any lunch,' he said, catching her glance. 'I always did have a sweet tooth—as you might remember.'

She shook her head, aware that she was being got at. He could say what he liked, he wasn't going to get a rise out of her. So far as she was concerned, the past was behind them. Humour struggled to surface for a moment, than sank again without a trace. There was nothing funny in this situation. Nothing at all!

'Don't look so grim,' he admonished, taking his seat beside her. 'We're over the worst.'

'I'd have thought this was the last job you'd have accepted, considering the circumstances,' she rejoined stonily. 'You can't be all that desperate for money.'

His shrug was easy. 'As I said, it was too good an offer to turn down. Japan is by way of being my second home. I lived over there as a boy. Didn't I ever tell you that?'

'You told me.' She gave him a straight and level glance. 'There's no point in talking about what happened two years ago, Greg. I'd as soon go on forgetting it.'

Blue eyes considered her speculatively. 'It was obvious the minute I walked through that door back there that you hadn't forgotten. Otherwise you wouldn't have gone to such pains to disguise the fact that we'd already met. Only let me put your mind at rest, Alex, my love. I took this job in spite of, not because of whom I was scheduled to work with. I don't have any designs on your body.'

Warm colour crept under her skin, but she kept her voice steady. 'So long as we understand each other.'

'Tolerate is the word.'

'I don't care what you call it. If we're going to spend the next two weeks in each other's pockets then it has to be a purely objective exercise. That means no snide references, no personal discussions of any kind. Agreed?'

'If you say so.' He sounded indifferent. 'Do you want me to pick you up on Monday?'

'Thanks, I'll make my own way to the airport.' She paused. 'Was there anything else you wanted to talk about?'

Broad shoulders lifted briefly. 'I guess not.'

'In that case we needn't prolong this.' She was rising as she spoke, control too close to slipping to risk another moment of contact. 'I'll see you at Heathrow.'

'You didn't drink your coffee,' he said.

'I know.' She didn't look at him. 'You have it for me.'

It was raining when she got outside. One of those swift summer showers out of a previously clear blue sky. There was no chance of finding a taxi free at this time of day, and she had no umbrella. The sensible thing to do would be to return to the shelter of the coffee-bar until the shower had passed, but right now nothing would have persuaded her to make that gesture. The nearest Tube station was about ten minutes' walk away. If she hurried she could make it without getting too wet.

Hurrying along the crowded pavements of home-going London was not easy. Before she had gone three hundred yards her light suit was soaked through on the shoulders and skirt front, her hair hanging in rats' tails about her face. She wasn't on her own. Lulled into a sense of security by the unbroken sunshine of the last few days, most people had been caught unawares. Not that it helped at all to know others were in the same boat. Rush hour on the Tube was going to be even less of a picnic than usual in this state, she reflected dismally.

She was looking for a gap in the traffic in order to save going all the way up to the crossing when one of the approaching cars drew into the kerb. Greg leaned across and thrust open the passenger door, ignoring the furious hooting of horns from those vehicles held up in line behind.

'Get in quick,' he advised. 'Before I get rammed!'

Her hesitation was brief. To refuse would have been childish in the extreme. The Underground terminal she had been making for was across the road, but there were others at which he could drop her. She slid into the car, yanking the door closed as they began moving again. Her hair was dripping down her front, the lapels of her linen suit were limp and curling, her pale beige shoes sodden wrecks.

'So much for the British summer!' she exclaimed in an attempt at lightness, too conscious of the picture she must present. 'Where did you have this stashed away?'

'Round the corner, on a meter.' He was concentrating on the traffic ahead. 'If you hadn't been in such an all-fired hurry to leave, I'd have offered you a lift.'

'If it weren't for the rain I'd have made the Underground by now,' Alex responded. 'You must have drunk your coffee quickly.'

A faint smile touched his lips. 'It was hardly worth drinking.'

'And the cake?'

'Dry as a bone.'

'Not your day, is it?' She couldn't quite conceal the malice. 'Not mine either, one way and another.'

'I've known worse.' He said it quietly, but with an underlying hardness that drew her eyes to his face. 'The day I came home and found that letter waiting for me, for instance.'

The muscles around her heart contracted painfully. 'I thought we were going to forget all that?'

'I'm not sure I want to forget it. You left a lasting impression on me, my love.'

'Stop calling me that!' Her voice was harsh. 'The only thing dented was your pride.'

'Not true, but I wouldn't expect you to understand deeper emotions. With you it was just a game.' There was a pause, a change of tone. 'How's your love-life these days?'

Alex took a grip on herself. He was simply trying to rile her—make her feel the guilty party. 'Thriving, thanks. How's yours?'

'Satisfactory.' He gave her a swift glance, his smile a taunt in itself. 'Life goes on.'

'Doesn't it.' She was looking ahead through the windscreen, trying to judge where they were. 'If you drop me off at this next corner I'll be fine. The rain's almost stopped.'

'You're still soaked,' he responded without making any attempt to pull over. 'My place is just a few minutes away. You can dry off there, then I'll take you home. Same place, is it?'

'No, it isn't. I live out in Wimbledon now.' She added jerkily, 'And quite apart from the fact that *your* place is nowhere near here, I've no intention of going there again—for any reason!'

'You're not the only one who's changed address,' he said. 'I found new studio premises, and converted the upper floor into a flat. The rates are astronomical, of course. Another reason why this job for *World* is attractive. The fee will help keep the LCC happy for another year—and I get a holiday into the bargain.'

'You're going there to work,' Alex retorted, momentarily side-tracked, 'not laze around!'

'When you love your work, every day is a holiday,' came the bland response. 'Obviously you don't feel the same way about yours.' He didn't wait for any reply. 'You're shivering. Want the heater on?'

She was trembling, not shivering, and it was nothing to do with being cold. She felt churned up inside, her peace of mind shattered. Greg still affected her; she couldn't deny that. It was necessary to keep reminding herself of what he was. If this coming trip was not to prove a total disaster, they had to find some basis of impartiality from which to work. Her future career could depend on it.

'Just a little,' she said. 'The temperature must have dropped ten degrees in the last half-hour.'

'I'd say the fine spell was over,' he agreed. 'You'll find it hot enough in Tokyo. Too much so if you catch a cold before you go. The sooner you're dried off, the better.'

There was too much sense in what he said to dispute the point. At least there would be no memories to contend with at the new premises. They were going to be in each other's company for a fortnight. They had to start somewhere.

'You've done very well for yourself, all told,' she remarked as he turned on to Kingsway.

'Been following my career?' he asked, and she bit her lip.

'Not deliberately. How come Ben knew you were *au fait* with Japanese culture?'

'We met at some function or other a couple of weeks ago. It came out in the course of conversation. I think I may even have sowed the seeds of the whole idea.'

'He only told me I'd got the job a few minutes before you arrived this afternoon,' Alex frowned. 'Yet you obviously knew beforehand.'

'No more than an hour or so. Up until he rang I'd had the idea it was going to be an all-male trip.'

Alex stole a glance at the lean profile. 'It must have been a shock for you.'

'Not nearly as much as it obviously was for you. I already knew you were with *World*. Anyone who reads the magazine would know. You've done pretty well for yourself too, if it comes to that.'

'Thanks.' She was hard put to it to sound gracious about it. 'After this job I hope to do even better.'

'I'm sure you will.' He took advantage of a momentary gap in the approaching traffic to whip across into one of the side-streets, a moment later angling the car through an archway to draw to a halt in a small, cobbled courtyard. 'My own little oasis,' he tagged on. 'It took some finding, and needed a hell of a lot of work, but it's worth every penny. The flat is up there,' indicating the iron-runged staircase running up the side of the building on the left. 'The studio front entrance is on Kingsway,' He was opening his door as he spoke. 'Let's get inside.'

Alex followed him up the staircase, waiting while he unlocked the heavy door. A stray shaft of sunlight glinted in the thick, dark hair as he bent his head to the task. She swallowed on the sudden dryness in her throat, remembering the crisp feel of it beneath her fingers, the way it would spring back on itself when she attempted to straighten out the faint kink. So many memories, and all of them emotive. She had loved this man so much— and hated him with an equal intensity. What she felt now went under neither guise, but it wasn't indifference. And therein lay the danger.

The small hallway had several doors leading off it. Greg led the way into a spacious living-room alive with colour and beautifully furnished. Deep chesterfields upholstered in creamy-white linen invited one to sink into their depths and contemplate the art studies grouped against dark red walls. On the far side of the room, three long, gracious windows looked down towards Aldwych.

'Nice,' was all Alex allowed herself. It was, she reflected privately, more than one step up from the place they had shared for those brief three months.

'I'll find you something to put on while those things dry,' said Greg from the doorway. 'Help yourself to a drink if you want one.'

There was a built-in bar across one corner of the room. Alex ignored it. She needed to keep a completely clear head. Greg returned bearing a white towelling robe with his initial monogrammed on the lower edge, handing it to her with a faint quirk of a lip. 'Present from a well-wisher,' he said. 'The bathroom is second door along, next to the kitchen. If you hand me out your things I'll put them in the dryer.'

'Every mod-con,' she observed. 'You do yourself proud!'

'My daily insists on it,' he returned equably. 'There's a hairdryer in there if you want to use it.'

The bathroom too was everything she might have anticipated. Both jacket and blouse were damp, her skirt badly creased where she had sat in it. She handed all three articles out to Greg without opening the door more than a few inches, then donned the robe, catching the faint tang of aftershave as she fastened the tie belt. He had used Estée Lauder when she had known him, she recalled. This smelled more like Halston. To please someone else's tastes, perhaps? The same one who had bought him this robe? Not Samantha Price, at any rate. The latter had married over a year ago and was living in New York.

So what did it have to do with her? she asked herself firmly at that point. He could have as many women as he wanted for all she cared!

He was in the small but superbly equipped kitchen when she eventually went out.

'I thought we might as well eat while we're waiting,' he said. 'Nothing elaborate. I'm not into *haute cuisine*. Chicken salad suit you?'

'Sounds fine,' Alex agreed. She stayed where she was in the doorway, leaning against the jamb to watch him take various dishes from the built-in refrigerator. 'You look quite domesticated.'

'Only in short bursts.' He had taken off his jacket and rolled up the sleeves of his shirt, revealing muscular forearms lightly covered in hair. Only on his chest did the hair grow thickly, Alex remembered: tight little whorls one could curl about a finger. She passed the tip of her tongue over dry lips, clamping down on the stirring within. That was all in the past, and it could stay there. The only relationship she and Greg were going to have was a working one.

He opened a bottle of wine to go with the meal, serving it out in the dining alcove off to one side of the main living-area. Cautious though she was in imbibing, Alex felt herself relaxing a little under the smooth influence. Greg kept the conversation strictly impersonal, talking about his years in Japan. His parents were retired and lived on Jersey, that much she knew. She had never met them. One didn't, she reflected cynically, introduce one's mistress to the family!

Looking at him now, it was difficult to imagine that firm, incisive mouth moving so softly against her own, those lean and clever hands caressing her body with such exquisite care. Life had been pretty wonderful those first weeks, she thought mistily, barely noticing that he had refilled her glass: the laughter, the fun, the excitement. She felt fired with sudden longing for all they might have had.

He was watching her with enigmatic expression, eyes too dark to penetrate. From somewhere she found the will-power to drag herself up and out of the trough of despondency into which she had sunk, to remind herself

of the two long years between then and now and regain
her hold on reality.

'May I see the new studio before I go?' she asked,
striving for a casual note.

'Why not?' He sounded casual himself. 'I don't have
anything to hide.'

She laughed. 'That makes two of us.'

'So I gathered,' he said, the irony so faint it could
have been imagined. 'If you hang your suit up before
we go downstairs, any creases will have dropped out by
the time you're ready to put it on again.'

'Good suggestion,' she agreed. 'I'll do that.'

The lower floor was reached via a door and narrow
staircase at the far end of the hallway. Greg switched on
lights to reveal a corridor off which lay one large and
one smaller studio, plus an office, two darkrooms, and
a small reception area for visiting clientele. He em-
ployed two assistants now, he told her, and a receptionist.

'Mandy's overriding ambition is to find a rich husband
and spend the rest of her life living it up in style,' he
added lightly. 'She's got the looks for it.'

'So why don't you marry her?' asked Alex, equally
lightly, and saw him smile.

'I'm neither rich enough or old enough for what she
has in mind. At twenty-two, she thinks the world's her
oyster.'

Unless someone came along and knocked all her plans
for six, reflected Alex on an edge of bitterness. She said
on a cooler note, 'I'd better be getting on home.'

He made no attempt to dissuade her. 'I'll drive you,'
he offered.

'No!' She took a grip on herself, tempering the refusal with a shrug and a shake of her head. 'Rush hour

is long over, and I doubt if it's going to rain again tonight. I'll take the Tube from Holborn. I can be up there in a few minutes.'

'Suit yourself.' He obviously didn't feel strongly enough about it to argue the point.

Her suit had hung out well enough to look decent. Even if it hadn't, Alex acknowledged, she still wouldn't be accepting the offer of a lift. Right now she wanted nothing more than to get away from Greg and all reminders of their past association. There was too much here that still had the power to hurt.

'See you at Heathrow, then,' he said at the door. He seemed remote, as if his mind had already moved on to other, more vital matters. 'Ben gave me both tickets. Maybe you'd better look after your own.'

Alex took it from him, steeling herself against any betraying quiver as their fingers touched. The job was all, she reflected grimly—a thought she was going to spend the weekend dinning into her mind. Two weeks wasn't all that long.

They flew the western route via Anchorage, Alaska, landing at Narita late morning of the following day.

Seen from the air, Tokyo was a vast megalopolis sprawling out in every direction from the grounds of the Imperial Palace, with the white-capped peak of Mount Fujiyama lofting beyond to a clear blue sky. From the ground it was much like any other aggressively modern, high-rise city, the roads bursting at the seams with traffic, the pavements thronged with hurrying, Western-clad pedestrians. Not that Alex had anticipated seeing kimonos worn on the city streets. Traditional garments would be reserved for the home, for leisure, for the country districts where progress had not yet encroached.

The hotel into which Greg had managed to book them was a mere stone's throw from the Imperial Palace itself. Flanked by stone dragons at the entrance, it was like entering another world. Outdoor shoes were exchanged in the front hallway for soft slippers, their baggage spirited away before Greg had finished signing in at the desk.

Waiting, Alex admired a superbly simple flower arrangement displayed in a niche, listening with half an ear to the quickfire and totally incomprehensible exchange between Greg and the man on Reception as the keys were handed over. It had been boiling hot outside, but in here the air was comfortably cool and fragranced. Peace reigned supreme.

It had been a long journey, though not an unpleasant one. Right now what she wanted most was a long soak in a warm tub and a change of clothing. The Japanese washed before getting into the bath, she recalled from the reading she had done this past couple of days, using the bath itself purely as a medium for relaxation. On reflection it seemed an excellent idea.

Greg had suggested a fairly quiet evening in order to overcome jet-lag. She couldn't quarrel with that either. He had been good company these past hours. Instructive, too; her notebook already had several pages filled. If they could keep up the same detachment from past relationships for the coming two weeks, things might not prove too bad after all. Afterwards, they could each go their own way with no regrets.

Simply and sparsely furnished, with cushions around a low table as the only immediately obvious items, the

room to which they were shown had a wall of sliding
glass screens overlooking a lovely inner garden, privacy
afforded by bamboo curtains which could be drawn
across at will. *Tatami* mats covered the floor, necessi-
tating the removal of even the slippers so as not to despoil
the pale surface of the dried, woven grasses. One needed,
Alex reflected fleetingly, immaculate hosiery or well-
pedicured feet to feel at ease in this country!

'I gather the bedrooms are separate?' she said as soon
as the kimono-clad maid had bowed herself from the
room again. 'And I do mean separate!'

Greg didn't turn a hair. 'This is it,' he said. 'The maid
will come in later and lay *futons* out for us on the floor.
That means mattress, by the way.' He gave her an oblique
glance before moving to pull screens covered in beautifully painted rice paper from hidden slots, effectively
chopping the room into two parts. 'There's your privacy,
but we share a bathroom. It's all they have—take it or
leave it. Only don't imagine you're going to find a room
anywhere else at this time of year.'

Alex bit her lip. She was in a cleft-stick, and he was
aware of it. His suggestion that they use a *ryoken* had
probably been made with just this situation in mind, she
fumed. The intimacy of such an arrangement was hardly
going to make detachment easy to achieve. Rice paper
was no barrier should he take it into his mind to attempt
a reconciliation of sorts.

'Don't concern yourself,' he advised drily, accurately
guessing her thoughts. 'As I said before, I don't have
any designs on your body. Do you want to take the
bathroom first, or shall I? They'll be serving our meal
in here in about an hour.'

Alex shrugged, forcing herself to accept the inevitable, though with serious reservations still. 'You go first. I'd like to unpack a few things.'

'You won't need your clothes tonight.' His lips widened into mockery at the expression that crossed her face. '*Yukata* are supplied fresh every day, along with the slippers we wear in the outer areas.' He was moving as he spoke, sliding back a section of the near wall to reveal a wardrobe-like recess from which he took blue and white cotton kimonos, handing the smaller of the two across to her. 'More comfortable than European wear, you'll find. You can sleep in it too.'

'Thanks.' Her tone was short. 'I have my own nightwear.'

Blue eyes regarded her with impatience. 'You're supposed to be plumbing the Japanese life-style. I'd have thought a little experimentation wouldn't go amiss.' His shrug dismissed the subject. 'I'm going to have that bath. I shouldn't bother doing too much unpacking. We're only going to be here a couple of nights.'

A couple of nights too long, she thought on a sudden edge of desperation. Being here in the close confines of this room with Greg was so different from the plane where they had been surrounded by other people. While he might be able to view her with total disinterest, she couldn't say the same of her own feelings regarding him. She only wished she could. In so many ways he was still the same man she had loved two years ago. She had to keep forcibly reminding herself of what he really was. The flat was obviously an all-male abode, but that wasn't to say he didn't have women friends visiting him there—even spending the night.

She could hear the splashing of a shower from the adjoining and surprisingly modern bathroom, a tuneless whistle. There was nowhere in the room to sit and relax, apart from the cushions themselves—nowhere even to rest her suitcase while she extracted her immediate needs from it. This was a different culture, she reminded herself. She wasn't here to criticise, only to observe.

Greg was wearing the *yukata* when he emerged from the bathroom. With his hair still damp and curling, he was heartrendingly familiar. Alex was glad of the excuse to get out of his way. The shower was separate from the tub. She left the latter to fill while she soaped and rinsed herself, throwing in a generous handful of fragrant salts before sliding into the warm water.

It felt delicious—the more so, she acknowledged, because she was already clean and could simply luxuriate. She let her mind drift, going over emerging impressions to create the opening paragraphs of the article that was going to send Ben into transports of delight and put her on the road to real journalistic stardom, with any luck. This job was her whole life, the only thing that mattered to her—the only thing she was going to allow to matter to her. Affect her though he still may, Greg was simply a passing distraction. All she had to do was recall the sound of Samantha's voice on the phone that night to harden her heart against him again.

The cotton kimono felt good against her skin, its simple design lacking in restriction. She felt oddly vulnerable without shoes or stockings. On impulse, she painted her toenails a delicate pink to match her fingers, waiting until they were dry enough to run no risk of leaving a trail of colour on the *tatami* before returning to the main room. Apart from a little moisturiser and a dab of lipstick, she left her face free of make-up. Greg was the last man she needed to put on a show for.

He was seated on one of the thin cushions at the table, looking through a magazine when she went out. The glance he ran over her revealed little of what he was thinking.

'Have some *sake*,' he invited, filling a porcelain cup from the flask on the table. 'Our food should be here any minute.'

Alex dropped awkwardly to a seat opposite him, tucking her legs under her. He looked so much at home, she thought, casting a surreptitious glance. The *yukata* had come open a little at the front, revealing the strong brown column of his throat and a dark triangle of hair. She had donned briefs beneath her own garment; she wondered if he had bothered.

Out of the corner of her eye she could see one long, muscular leg stretched comfortably out, the material fallen away to above knee level. Her heart felt as if it were hammering into her throat, her stomach muscles so taut they hurt. She took a sip of the hot *sake*, gasping as the alcohol hit her throat. Almost immediately she was aware of a slight lessening of tension, of a pleasant glow. It was going to be all right, she thought. Everything was going to be just fine!

Night had descended outside. With the bamboo blinds drawn back one could look straight out across the subtly floodlit gardens to the opposite curve of the building where one or two other rooms were also on view. A group of men sat around one table, all of them dressed in the same cotton house garments. The sound of voices and hearty male laughter floated across. Next door to them, a young couple stood in their opened doorway, arms about each other in total oblivion. Watching, Alex felt like a voyeur. She also felt a sharp envy.

'Love's young dream,' commented Greg, following her eyes. 'The same the world over. They're probably on honeymoon—blind to everything else but each other!'

'Don't mock it,' she responded tautly. 'Just because you don't believe in true love, it doesn't have to follow that it doesn't exist.'

One dark eyebrow lifted. 'Who said I don't believe in it? It's all a matter of meeting the right person.'

Alex levelled her voice with an effort. 'From which I gather that you haven't, so far?'

'Clever deduction. Not that I've given up hope. It springs eternal.'

'Good for you.' She stirred restlessly. 'I hope the food isn't going to be long.'

'Have some more *sake* to be going on with,' he invited, refilling her cup. 'There's no hurry—for anything.'

She slanted a swift glance, but there was nothing in his expression to suggest innuendo. She was reading too much into too little again, she warned herself, and it had to stop.

'In this country,' he said now, 'it's regarded as polite to pour other people's drinks for them.' He held up his cup towards her, eyes glinting in the soft lamplight. 'So do your duty.'

Stifling the urge to tell him where he got off, Alex reached out a hand and lifted the flask, filling the cup until it was on the point of brimming over. 'Enough?' she enquired in silky tones.

'Just about.' The glint had become a gleam, infinitely disturbing. 'Acting the bitch isn't going to improve matters.'

She laughed, suddenly uncaring. 'I didn't even get started yet! You know your trouble, Greg? You're arrogant. You always were! You took this job to pay me out, didn't you? You hoped I'd miss out on the chance because I wouldn't dare risk being on my own with you out here. Well, you were wrong, and now you're stuck with it. I find that very amusing!'

He carried the brimming cup to his lips without spilling a drop and substantially lowered the level before stating flatly, 'I'm not going to argue with you. And I shouldn't have any more of that if I were you. Drink always did go to your head too fast. I should have remembered.'

'Look to your own interests,' she retorted, and promptly drained the cup, setting it down again with a thud and a challenging glitter. 'You don't worry me, Greg. Not in any fashion! Setting *this* up...' with a disparaging sweep of a hand around the room '...won't get you anywhere!'

'That rather depends,' he said, 'on where it is I want to get.' His gaze had hardened. 'Don't push too hard, or you might just make it over the top. I operate on a shorter fuse these days.'

A knock on the outside door heralded the entry of the same young woman who had brought them to the room earlier. She was bearing a tray holding several dishes, which she proceeded to set out on the table at Greg's invitation. Alex listened as he spoke to the girl in her own language, horribly conscious that she had come close to making a fool of herself. The *sake* was dynamite, she thought, feeling the room spin then steady again. And Greg was right: she had never had much of a head for alcohol of any kind. Knocking it back that way had been an idiotic gesture. The problem now being that the effect wasn't going to go away just because she regretted the cause.

The first dish was egg noodle soup, eaten, Alex was thankful to note, with a porcelain spoon. It was delicious, though if anything it seemed only to increase the effects of the *sake*. Greg showed her how to manipulate the chopsticks, which were shorter and therefore a little more manageable than the Chinese variety. They each of them had a personal dish of the basic *kake*, which consisted of soft noodles cooked in *bouillon* and served with a side plate of spices and shredded leeks, dipping into the various other bowls as and when the fancy took them.

Much of what Alex tried to pick out finished up on the table, not least because her eyes were refusing to focus properly. She longed for a knife and fork, inwardly cursing the day when she had agreed to take this job; cursing Greg for being there with her, so superior in his total familiarity with these outlandish ways. No proper beds, no proper eating implements—and, no matter how she tried to position them, her legs kept getting cramped. Two whole weeks of this was going to be an endurance test out of all proportion to the rewards of the job. She would fly back tomorrow, tell Ben to find someone else to write his precious feature!

'Not having a lot of success, are you?' said Greg drily.

He pressed himself to his feet, coming round behind her to take her hand and reposition the chopsticks, keeping his fingers on hers while he guided her into picking up a fried shrimp and transferring it to her mouth. She could feel his breath on the nape of her neck where the hair had parted, the warmth of his body at her back. She knew a sudden longing to lean into his shoulder, to have his arms slide around her, to feel his lips caress the soft skin just below her ear, the way they used to do, moving down to push aside the thin cotton of her robe and follow the line of her shoulderbone, so light and yet so stirring.

Perhaps something of her emotions was communicated to him, because he seemed to stiffen a little, letting go of her to sit back on his heels.

'Think you can manage now?' he asked.

'Yes.' Her voice felt strangled. 'Thanks.'

'Don't mention it.' The taunt was back, if a fraction more edged. 'If you're going to see this thing through, it has to be wholesale. Otherwise there's no point. I'll remember not to offer you *sake* in future. That should help.'

Across the way, the young lovers had closed their blinds, shutting themselves off from the outside world. Alex wished blindly that she could do the same. Had she realised just how difficult this trip was going to be she would never have come, job or no job. There were things more important to her at this precise moment than a career.

The meal ended with coffee, too strong for Alex's tastes. Without being asked, the maid brought out rolled mattresses and bedding from another of the wall cupboards and laid them out side by side in the other half of the room. It was going to be too warm for blankets, thought Alex, watching her.

The effects of the *sake* were beginning to wear off, leaving her listless and bone-weary. Jet-lag, she told herself, trying to keep her eyes open long enough to see the maid out of the room so that she could drag her own *futon* this side of the sliding doors. Tomorrow she could start over, the way she meant to go on. Tomorrow...

CHAPTER THREE

A MUTED light was filtering into the room through drawn blinds when Alex awoke. She could hear bird-song, sweet and clear, underscored by the faint sound of voices.

This was Japan, she remembered. Tokyo, to be precise. The disorientation gave way to a throbbing headache as she sat up, making her wince. Her mouth was so dry, her lips felt stuck together. She ran the tip of her tongue over them, grimacing at the taste. This was no way to start a new day. Especially when there was going to be so much to fit in. A shower, and half a tube of toothpaste, might help a little. Certainly nothing could make her feel worse!

It was only when she turned her head and saw the other mattress right beside hers that realisation dawned. Greg had slept there, so close that had she rolled in the night she would have been sharing a bed with him. Perhaps she had, came the thought, causing her heart to miss a beat. The last thing she remembered with any clarity at all was watching the maid gather up the dishes from the table before departing.

She was still wearing the *yukata*. That, in itself, was reassuring. Apart from which, Greg was hardly the type to take advantage of a drunken stupor. Not quite fair to herself either, she acknowledged wryly. The *sake* had been aided and abetted by her jet-lag; it was probably going to take a couple of days to adjust.

She had never really stopped caring; she knew that now. The emotion had simply been held in limbo. There had been no one else since, apart from the odd date. Yet feeling this way altered nothing. He had had an affair with Samantha Price. If she had stayed with him, how many more might there have been?

The bathroom door opened and Greg came out. He was shaved, and wearing trousers and casual shirt, his feet bare.

'Morning,' he said. 'Sleep well?'

Alex eyed him for a moment without answering, grappling with her inner self. Want him she might, trust him she couldn't, and they still had to get through the coming two weeks.

The mobile left eyebrow lifted. 'Cat got your tongue?'

'That's more or less what it feels like,' she admitted ruefully. 'I think I sprouted a fur rug!'

'Shame.' He sounded surprisingly sympathetic. 'Usually it's only cheap *sake* that causes ill effects. Try a cold shower, and drink plenty of water. You'll be fine again in half an hour.'

Alex doubted it. Without meaning to, she said, 'You didn't move the mattresses last night.'

'It hardly seemed worth the trouble.' He had gone to squat in front of his open suitcase, his back turned to her: a strong back, tapering from broad shoulders down to narrow waist and hip, the latter outlined by the taut stretch of his trousers. 'I went out like a light myself not five minutes after putting you down.'

'You carried me?' The question came sharp.

'Sure, I carried you.' The dark head swung her way, mouth curved in faint mockery. 'It was either that or leave you where you keeled over.'

She coloured. 'I made an idiot of myself, didn't I?'

'No more than many a one before you. *Sake* is insidious; it creeps up on you. I should have known better.'

'Except that you couldn't be expected to realise I was still so susceptible.'

The blue eyes took on a more vivid hue for a moment. 'Some things don't change. Are you going to get up? Breakfast will be here in about ten minutes.'

Alex thrust back the sheet, forcing nonchalance. The intimacy of this arrangement left little room for bashfulness. Greg had seen her first thing in the morning before—and wearing far less than she was wearing right now. Why let it bother her? It obviously didn't bother him.

The cold shower went a long way towards restoring her to normal. With teeth cleaned, and the foul coating brushed vigorously from her tongue, she felt ready to face whatever the day threw at her.

Clad in white cotton slacks and sleeveless top, she went back to the main room to find breakfast already laid out ready for consumption. Greg had the sliding doors open to the fresh air and the masterpiece of a garden with its dwarfed trees and shrubs, and tinkling waterfalls. The young honeymooners were strolling together, a decorous distance between them.

'So what's on the agenda for today?' she asked brightly, lowering herself on to a cushion. Her smile faded as she viewed the array of food on offer. There was rice, pickles, a kind of soup, slivers of raw fish and a dish of some dark vegetable not unlike dried spinach. Her stomach did a quick flip, then settled again, although the longing for a lightly boiled egg remained.

'Seaweed,' Greg supplied, anticipating the question. 'Try it, it's good.'

'I'll take your word for it,' she said. She eyed the glass of thick yellowish liquid he had to one side. 'What's that?'

'Raw egg beaten in milk. One of the best pick-me-ups I know of.' He studied her with amusement. 'You have to eat something.'

'Not right now I don't.' Reaching for the small beautifully decorated tea-kettle, she filled one of the handleless cups, looking askance at the green liquid. It was certainly different, she found, on forcing herself to taste it, but oddly refreshing.

'We'll call in at one of the European hotels and find you something more to your taste,' offered Greg. 'Give you a chance to see where the average tourist stays at the same time. I thought we might make a start with the Ginza. It's a good place to do any personal shopping while we're about it.'

'You're a great believer in this killing two birds with the one stone!' Alex derided, and received an unmoved glance.

'I don't believe in wasting time, no. Later on we'll be visiting a *kabuki* theatre, then tomorrow...' He paused there, shaking his head. 'No use counting on anything. It all depends on Yuki.'

'What is *yuki*?' Alex asked.

'Who,' he corrected. 'She's a lady with a lot of clout in the right places. A daughter of one of Honshu's oldest families. We're having dinner at her apartment.'

Alex lifted expressive brows. 'Not a traditional daughter, then?'

He ignored the sarcasm. 'Yuki's what you might call a modern progressive. Luckily her people were progressive enough themselves to allow her that much freedom.'

'Lucky Yuki!' She made a show of looking at her watch. 'Shouldn't we be making a move? It's gone eight-thirty.'

'You're fast,' he said. 'I make it quarter-past. Why don't you take a short stroll in the garden while I sort my camera case? I don't want to be carrying any unnecessary weight around.'

A short stroll was all it could be, Alex reflected, considering the restricted area, but she accepted the suggestion anyway, sliding her feet into flat-heeled sandals before stepping down from the open window on to the narrow path that skirted the perimeter. Although the sun was not yet quite high enough to clear the eastern side of the building, the heat and humidity smote her like a tangible weight, creating instant stickiness. What it was going to be like in the city itself she hated to think.

Despite the limited space, the landscaping was intricate, with streams and waterfalls and winding paths all converging on a natural pool. A curved bamboo bridge spanned the water. Leaning on the side rail, Alex counted fifteen huge golden carp. She was still engrossed in watching them when Greg called her name, looking up to hear the click as he operated the camera shutter from a short distance away.

'You're not here to waste film,' she said shortly, too conscious of his dark attraction as he stood there smiling that enigmatic smile of his. 'I'd have thought you'd need all you've brought.'

'I can always buy more,' he returned. 'It was a good shot. I thought you might like it for your album.'

'I don't keep one.' She came down from the bridge, avoiding his eyes. 'Ready, are we?'

'As we'll ever be.' He touched her arm, indicating the path to the right. 'We'll go out through the gate over there, then we don't have to remove shoes again.'

Once outside in the narrow street they were back in the twentieth century. Right around the corner, the snack bar of a modern, high-rise hotel provided the coffee and toast that was all Alex wanted. The place was swarming with tourists of all nationalities, the parade of in-house boutiques and gift shops already bursting at the seams. Had it not been for the oriental features of the staff, who all wore European clothing, they could, Alex acknowledged, be almost anywhere in the world. Most of those staying here would never know the Japan she had come to find. Certainly few of them would experience a *ryoken* unless they spoke the language as well as Greg did. It gave her a certain sense of superiority.

Standing within its own parkland, like a giant traffic island in the centre of the city, the Imperial Palace was pretty much hidden from view among trees in full leaf. No visitors were allowed inside those gates unless expressly invited, Greg advised, and such invitations were rare enough to be virtually non-existent. Foreign journalists were *persona non grata* with the Emperor anyway, he added; photographers even more so. The Imperial family must remain uncontaminated by Western culture.

'Unless you want to risk a night drop over the wall to get a close-up picture,' he suggested in the taxi heading for the Ginza district. 'I'm not sure what the penalty might be if caught. Beheading, probably. These people don't mess about.'

Alex controlled a shudder, not sure whether to take him seriously or not. He looked so cool, so untouched by the heat, while already she could feel herself wilting. Looking out of the taxi window as the vehicle waited for traffic lights to change, she saw a young woman in a beautifully embroidered kimono poised on the pavement edge. Thick black shining hair was coiled in traditional fashion about her small and shapely head, with a lotus flower held in place by a fragile pearl comb. Her make-up was very pale, almost white, emphasising the almond eyes, the red bow of a mouth.

'*Geisha,*' Greg supplied. 'Probably on her way to a luncheon appointment. She'll act as the hostess for a group of businessmen.'

'I thought clients were supposed to visit them,' Alex murmured, still fascinated by the sight.

'It works both ways. Visiting the house is more expensive.'

She cast an oblique glance. 'You've done it yourself?'

'I've been taken a couple of times. It's a great honour to be invited to spend an evening in the "flower and willow world".' His smile held a familiar hint of mockery. 'High-class entertainment by Japanese standards, a little boring by mine. I prefer the less esoteric when it comes to female companionship.'

'More physical than philosophical, you mean?' suggested Alex blandly. 'That figures!'

He laughed. 'I don't pretend to understand the female mind. Few men can. Take yourself as a case in point. For weeks you acted a part you supposedly found obnoxious. I'm still wondering why you bothered.'

Their driver had his attention fixed on road and radio. It was doubtful, Alex thought, if he understood English anyway. None the less, she lowered her voice. 'We're supposed to be forgetting all that.'

'You're making it difficult.' His regard was speculative. 'I might not be so hot on what makes your mind work, but I can still recognise a come-on when I see it. You wanted me last night, Alex.'

Her whole body felt tense as a bowstring. From somewhere she found the ability to shrug. 'Modesty was never your strong point. If I wanted *anything* last night it was sleep. And, while we're on the subject, I'd prefer it if you laid your *futon* the other side of the room tonight!'

'Tell the maid, not me,' came the infuriating retort. 'Or move your own, if it means so much to you. It's all the same to me.'

Meaning she was safe enough anyway, Alex concluded, and felt a dull ache in her chest. Whatever hold she might once have had on him, it was gone for good now. He couldn't have made that clearer. Better that way, of course—if she could only teach her senses to stop reacting to his every move.

Afternoon was drawing towards evening when they finally returned to the *ryoken* in order to bathe and change their clothing. Shattered by the heat, by the crowds, by the sheer amount of material already gathered, Alex would willingly have forgone the dinner engagement with Greg's Japanese friend in order to spend a quiet evening pulling her ideas together.

The Ginza had been fascinating, from the huge stores and smart specialist shops of the main streets through to the maze of narrow back streets lined with smaller shops, bars and restaurants where delivery vans, scooters and pedestrians battled for right of way. The time they had spent in the *kabuki* theatre, watching wonderfully garbed players portraying the conflict between duty and true love that appeared to be the central theme of all Japanese plays, had left her ears ringing with the discordant sounds that passed for music in this part of the world. An acquired taste, Greg had acknowledged, unsympathetic towards her growing restlessness. Granted permission to take photographs, he had insisted on seeing the performance through to the bitter end.

'Yuki is looking forward to meeting you,' he stated when Alex tentatively suggested he went on alone. The blue eyes had a hard look about them. 'She'll have gone to a lot of trouble. You're not going to let her down.'

'If she means *that* much to you,' she said with deliberation, 'I'd have thought you'd welcome a chance to be on your own with her. The progressives surely don't have need of a chaperon?'

Greg ignored the sally. 'Just be ready by seven-thirty,' he said. 'That gives you almost an hour.'

Taking a look at the set of his jaw, Alex decided against arguing about it. His relationship with the Japanese girl was something she didn't want to think about too deeply. That he should be so concerned for her feelings suggested rather more than the casual friendship she had first assumed, although as he hadn't been here in Japan for more than a year there could hardly be anything serious between them.

And if there was, what was it to do with her? she asked herself hardily. Last night, even this morning, she had been remembering the man she had once thought him to be. Only he wasn't and never could be that man again.

She wore a silk blouse and skirt in turquoise and white, sliding her feet into strappy sandals as soon as they reached the outer doors. Greg was devastating in an off-white lightweight suit with a dark blue shirt open at the throat beneath. He had gone to a lot of trouble, Alex thought hollowly, and it certainly wasn't for her benefit.

The modern apartment block in which Yuki lived was situated in the Chiyoda ward of the city. Deposited on the seventh floor by the cramped lift, Alex took a look out of the landing window at the sparkling lights. The soaring silhouette of the Tokyo tower some half-mile or so away lent the scene a Parisian look. Beyond it, the city seemed to stretch to the distant horizon.

Yuki Nagasowa opened the apartment door to them. Not the girl Alex had somehow imagined she would be, but a woman in her late twenties, poised and lovely in a delicately patterned white dress. Her eyes lit up on seeing Greg, her kiss of greeting purely Western in its connotations.

'It has been so long!' she said in excellent English. The smile she directed at Alex was apologetic. 'You must make allowances for my enthusiasm. Greg is an old and dear friend.'

Don't mind me, Alex wanted to say, but thought better of it. From the way Greg was smiling, the pleasure was entirely mutual.

'Not that old,' he said, drawing a quicksilver laugh. 'The nuances of your language escape me still, it seems!'

They were not, Alex found, to dine alone. The two men and one woman already present in the compact living-room came to their feet as the newcomers entered, bowing low on introduction. All three were dressed in

Western fashion, and all, she was thankful to find, spoke English, though with varying degrees of proficiency.

Yuki, she learned over the course of the evening, was a lecturer in languages at the university. Not a common achievement for a Japanese female, she gathered. Despite the apparent Westernisation of the four, the atmosphere was far more formal than she would have anticipated. When anyone spoke, all listened attentively, nodding their heads like so many mandarins in unison with each word. At one point Alex found herself following suit, and hastily stopped it in case they thought she was mocking them. None of them ever openly disagreed with a statement, but would find some other way of conveying a difference of opinion. It was, she privately thought, carrying politeness to extremes!

Greg seemed perfectly at home. He was knocking back *sake* as though there was no tomorrow, she thought sourly. She made hers last, shaking her head with a smile when Yuki urged her to a refill.

'I find it too potent,' she declared, refusing to glance in Greg's direction. 'I'm quite happy with the tea.'

'You must take Alex to a tea-ceremony, Greg,' said Yuki. 'But not the ones put on for the tourists, of course. I will make the arrangements in Kyoto.'

'What about the other thing?' he asked. 'No luck?'

Her smile was accompanied by an apologetic shrug. 'It is not a simple matter to arrange. Perhaps in Kyoto again it can be done. My mother may be able to help.'

'If she can't, no one can,' he agreed. 'We'll be leaving tomorrow afternoon. When do you plan to travel?'

'Perhaps the next day, but only for one week. I have my private students to consider.'

Greg inclined his head. 'One week of your company is worth a thousand days!' he declared extravagantly, drawing appreciative laughter and murmurs of approbation from those about him.

Yuki's mouth curved. 'We shall make a Japanese of you yet, Wilde *san*!'

It was only when they were in the taxi going back to the *ryoken* that Alex voiced the question.

'What is it Yuki is supposed to be arranging for us?'

'A visit to a *geisha* house,' Greg acknowledged. 'I thought a look at the kind of training a *geisha* has to undergo might be useful to you. That's where the difficulty comes in. European women have no place in that kind of establishment.'

Alex made no effort to keep the tartness out of her voice. 'Hardly surprising. Why should her mother be able to help?'

'Because she was a *geisha* herself before she married Haruo.' The sideways glance was lacking in tolerance. 'And before you assume anything, that in no way means he married a call girl. A *geisha* trained the traditional way is regarded as something special in this country. Misako certainly is!'

Something inside Alex refused to withdraw. 'I'll take your word for it.'

'You'd darn well better!' He sounded curt himself. 'You suggest any different in this feature of yours and I'll personally sue the damned magazine for defamation!'

'I'll write it the way I see it,' she declared with heat. 'You're here to take photographs, not tell me how to do my job—Wilde *san*!'

His laugh was sudden and unexpected. 'A bit of the green-eye creeping in, is it? Yuki too much woman for you?'

'Go to the devil,' she said thickly, too well aware that he had a valid point. Looks, brains, personality—Yuki had it all. The relationship between the two of them was still not clear. More than mere friends for certain, but how much more?

The room they were to share for another night seemed more confining than ever. Once again their mattresses had been laid side by side. Alex lost no time in seizing hold of hers and dragging it to a new position on the far side of the sliding doors. When she straightened, Greg was right behind her, his eyes glittering with an emotion allied to anger as he took hold of her by the shoulders.

'If this is what you're so bloody afraid of, let's get it out of the way,' he clipped.

The kiss was searing, reminiscent of that other time in its expression of contempt. Alex fought it, but he was too strong for her, holding her still with a hand clamped about the back of her neck. She could feel the lean length of him hard against her, the taut muscles of his thighs—sense the moment when the anger began to give way to something else. Despite herself, she softened, began to answer. It was Greg himself who did the thrusting away, mouth curled.

'No way, sweetheart. I've been down that road before!'

Too often, she thought, already regretting the brief response. 'You started it,' she flung back. 'Just leave me alone, Greg!'

'Then don't needle me into it.' He was in control of himself again, derision in his eyes. 'If you're going short of a man these days, the fault can only be yours.'

'I'm not,' she flared, then bit her lip, aware of the trap he had set for her.

'So there is someone? Special, is he?'

She said bitterly, 'More than you ever were!'

'That I don't doubt.' He turned away, his back conveying dismissal. 'We'd better get some sleep. We'll need an early start in the morning if we want to do the Meiji Shrine before taking the train to Kyoto.'

For a fleeting moment she was tempted to fling the accusation after him, to see that indifference torn from him, but only for a moment. What was the use? He'd only deny it. She would be the one to lose out.

Surrounded by mountains, Kyoto was a mixture of the old and the new, with modern apartment blocks standing cheek by jowl with traditional buildings.

The Nagasowa family lived in an area called Ichijoji on the eastern slopes, their home a lovely, pagoda-roofed old place set in its own landscaped grounds. Haruo Nagasowa was perhaps in his mid-sixties, his wife Misako a good ten years younger. They both spoke fairly good English, and were sufficiently well versed in Western ways to adopt the first-name mode of address rather than the more formal *san*. Yuki, it appeared, was their only child.

The house was built to a traditional pattern in which many interior walls consisted only of heavy rice paper stretched over a wooden frame. The bathroom was a later addition at the rear of the building, built around a small hot spring and obviously a source of great pride to Misako. There was space for three or four people to share the natural pool with its shelves and ledges formed by cooling minerals. To one side was a modern shower for the mandatory cleansing before the relaxing soak.

As in the *ryoken*, the room which the guests were to use for sleeping purposes had a sliding screen divider down the middle which could be drawn at will, each half having separate entry from the central hall.

'A tactful way of catering to our Western moralities,' Greg commented drily when they were alone. 'The choice is ours to make.'

'One thing we don't have to consider,' Alex retorted, and drew a measured glance.

'About that I'm not so sure any more. Maybe I was a mite too quick turning down the offer last night. You've still got what it takes.'

Green eyes flared. 'There was no *offer*!'

'That's not how it felt at the time. I could have taken you all the way without too much effort.'

'Like hell!' she snapped.

The smile was slow, calculated to a degree. 'Hot, I'll grant you. You'll probably find a *yukata* in the cupboard over there. You've got half an hour before I take my bath.'

He was playing games with her, Alex told herself as he slid the screen across between them. He had no more intention than she had of furthering last night's mistake. The knowledge that he awoken a part of her which she had thought, if not dead, at least under control, was something she didn't want to think about too deeply.

Although not as humid as in Tokyo, the temperature was still in the upper seventies. Alex was glad of the cool cotton next to her skin when she slid into the *yukata* after a quick shower. Misako took her to look at the garden while they waited for the men to join them.

'It is nothing,' she deprecated in typical Japanese fashion, 'but there is little else to show you that you

would find interesting.' There was a pause before she
added with obvious reticence, 'One thing I must tell you.
In Japan, only the dead wear their kimonos folded right
over left the way you have done.'

'Oh, how awful!' Alex was quick to rectify the matter,
looking up again with rueful expression. 'I'm so sorry,
Misako.'

'You could not have known,' the other returned, and
then with anxiety, 'You do not mind that I say it?'

'Of course not,' Alex hastened to assure her. 'I'd have
been far more mortified if you hadn't and then I'd found
out later.' She made a small wry gesture. 'It probably
isn't the only thing I'm going to get wrong while I'm in
your country.'

'Greg knows our ways.' She pronounced the name a
little self-consciously, leaving Alex with the impression
that in her heart of hearts she felt more at home with
the old ways. 'He will tell you what is important.' There
was a delicate question in the almond eyes. 'You are more
to him, I think, than just a colleague?'

Something inside Alex drew the words from her. 'We
used to live together.'

There was more puzzlement than censure in the glance
the other woman slanted towards her. 'Not now?'

'No.' Alex bent to touch the petals of a huge scarlet
poppy. 'We had a misunderstanding.'

'Ah!' Misako's tone took on enlightenment. 'Between
men and women it is often so. I would have offered you
another room had I known. It is just that Yuki said...'
She broke off, shaking her head as if in self-admonition.
'The position can be altered.'

Not for anything, Alex reflected, was she going to have
Greg thinking she had asked to be moved away from

him. He would only take it that she was afraid to have
him close. 'There's no need to go to that trouble,' she
said. 'We can manage.'

'As you would prefer.' The Japanese woman's
expression was inscrutable. 'Shall we return to the house?
It grows cool.'

Greg and Haruo were already seated at the table which
occupied a central position in the spacious living-room,
glasses of the Japanese beer to hand. Alex asked for tea
when offered a choice, earning an approving nod from
her host and a jeering little smile from Greg, which latter
she ignored.

Served by one of the two elderly women who constituted the staff, the meal was many-coursed, every dish
beautifully prepared. It took courage on Alex's part to
try the thinly sliced raw fish which the others obviously
found so appetising, and she couldn't in all honesty say
she cared very much for it. She was beginning to yearn
for a good old-fashioned meat pie with crusty pastry
and hot brown gravy.

'Yuki telephoned this morning to say you have a wish
to see a *geisha* house,' said Misako unexpectedly after
they had left the men to enjoy their conversation and
retired to the covered terrace. 'It will not be a simple
matter to arrange, but I will do what I can. Foreigners
to our country so often misunderstand what it is that a
geisha does.'

'I have a completely open mind,' Alex assured her.
She added carefully, 'You were one yourself, I
understand?'

'That is so. I entered the *okiya* when I was twelve years.
I was seventeen years before I began repaying my debt,
and twenty-five when I married Haruo.' Her tone was

reminiscent. 'I regret no part of those years. They taught me so much.' She laughed. 'Although I must confess that my conversation no longer holds Haruo's attention the way it did when he was paying to hear it! He has been a good husband,' she added swiftly, as if conscious of some implied criticism. 'There is none better!'

Alex murmured an appropriate reply, thinking bleakly that if Greg had only been the man he had at first appeared to be she might by now have been in a position to make the same claim. It had been so good between them at first. Not just in lovemaking, but in everyday companionship too. It just went to show how little one ever really knew of another person's inner self.

No objection was raised when she opted to retire at ten in order to write up her notes. Misako took the same option, leaving the two men to finish their beer and conversation. It seemed an age before Greg came to bed. Alex listened to the sound of movement from beyond the drawn screens, heard him lie down on the *futon*, and resolutely turned her attention back to the words she had written during this past hour.

They lacked both sparkle and originality, she knew. Ben was going to expect insight as well as visual description from this feature. If she couldn't supply it there would be no further opportunities on offer.

Greg couldn't be allowed to rob her of this opportunity, she thought with determination. It meant too much to her. She had to teach herself to disregard him.

CHAPTER FOUR

ALEX spent a restless night. By six o'clock there seemed little point in prolonging the exercise. Moving quietly, she gathered her things and slipped out through the side screen to make for the bath house. At this hour she was unlikely to be disturbed by anyone.

It was the work of a few minutes to take a shower before entering the main pool. The water was deliciously warm, the smell of sulphur too weak to create a problem. Resting on one of the lower ledges, Alex closed her eyes and tried to relax her mind along with her body. By the time she saw Greg again she wanted to be in total control of both physical and mental responses. That was the only way she was going to get through the coming days.

Today was Friday already. Their return flight was booked for a week the following Monday. Not so very long. After they left Kyoto she would insist they checked into a European-style hotel with more conventional sleeping arrangements.

'Finding it beneficial?' asked a too-familiar voice, and she opened her eyes to find the subject of her thoughts looking down at her from the side of the pool. From this angle, with the *yukata* loosely wrapping his body, he seemed to tower. His mouth quirked as she stared at him. 'You should have put a notice on the door.'

'Would it have kept you out?' she asked tautly, finding her voice again.

'That would have depended on what it said.' His eyes followed the lines of her body, only partially cloaked by the water. 'Sleep well, did you?'

Her own robe lay over a stand several feet away. Short of getting out of the water to reach it, she had no way of avoiding that scrutiny. 'Fine,' she said. 'And you?'

'Fitfully,' he acknowledged. 'I think I must have been suffering from frustration.'

She brought herself upright in the water, trying not to rush the movement. 'Yuki will be here tonight. Perhaps she'll oblige.'

'Leave her name out of it.' He hadn't raised his voice but the inflection was harder. 'This is between you and me.'

The open shower was right in her line of vision. Stripping off the *yukata*, he stepped beneath the flow and reached for the soap. He boasted no single ounce of spare and flabby flesh, his stomach muscles as taut and flat as they had always been. She had known that the other night, of course, but only on a tactile level. She felt her own muscles spasm suddenly, the warmth beginning to curl through her. Damn him, she thought desperately. Why couldn't he leave her alone?

The shower was turned off. With measured, unhurried strides, he came over to let himself down into the pool, eyes jeering as they rested on her face.

'Anyone would think it was the first time you'd seen me without any clothes on,' he commented. 'Relax. That's what this place is for.'

'Is that the way Misako is likely to see it if she knows we've been in here together?' Alex responded on a caustic note. 'I thought mixed bathing was frowned on these days?'

'In public, mostly. In private it's a personal choice.'

'Between consenting adults, you mean.'

The sarcasm failed to stir him. 'Something like that. Those who bathe together stay together. Maybe we should have done more of it ourselves while we had the chance.'

He was bare feet away; too close, Alex acknowledged, for comfort. She said huskily, 'It wouldn't have made any difference in the long run.'

'Meaning your boredom threshold would have remained about the same.' Body supported by the shelf beneath his back, he rolled his head to look at her. 'I still have that letter you left me. I thought of having it framed at one time. The trouble with you, Alex, is you only want what you haven't got.' The pause was a taunt in itself. 'Well, after due consideration, I've decided to indulge both of us. Why cut my nose off to spite my face?'

'I'm getting out!' she stated, unable to hear any more.

'Not unless I move out of the way, you're not,' he said. 'And I'm not prepared to do that . . . yet.'

She subsided again, looking at him helplessly. 'What good is this going to do?'

'Call it a small recompense. You still stir the blood, darling, even if you are a bitch!'

'Maybe I'd good reason to be one,' she flung back. 'Did that ever occur to you?'

'So tell me,' he invited.

She damped down the impulse with an effort. Better he should go on believing what he did believe than give him the satisfaction of knowing just how hard he had hit her. This way she at least stayed on top.

'Work it out for yourself,' she said flatly.

He laughed. 'No back-up? How like a woman!'

One hand reached for her, grasping her wrist to pull her closer. The water made resistance difficult. Alex felt his knee graze her bare thigh, then she was hard up against him, his arms trapping her with a strength and purpose she couldn't fight.

His mouth had no brutality, just a seeking determination to make her respond. And respond she did, despite everything, trembling at the swift run of heat through her body at the feel of him. For the moment it ceased to matter why he was kissing her, just so long as he kept right on doing it. It was like coming back to life again after being in suspended animation.

There was a slight roughness in his voice when he came up for air at last. 'Still the same little passion flower! You surprised me with that the very first time we made love. Remember the occasion?'

'I remember,' she said unsteadily. 'I remember it *all*, Greg. Every damned minute! If there's one thing I learned this past two years it's that there's more to life than just being good in bed!'

His smile mocked her. 'An ambiguous statement if ever I heard one!' He released her then without apparent regret. 'Time we were moving. There's a lot to get through.'

The whole episode had been conducted with deliberation, thought Alex achingly as he slid from the pool. If he had been wearing a sleeve he would have been laughing up it at the ease with which he had roused her to acknowledge him. It mustn't happen again; she couldn't afford for it to happen again. Not when her every sense warned of the danger in any further contact.

They spent the greater part of the day doing a tourist's round of the city and its environs, taking in several of the many fine temples, exploring Nijo Castle with its palaces and gardens and finishing up on one of the observation platforms of the Tower building for an overall view.

Kyoto was a city of contrasts, from the huge fourteenth-century Zen Buddhist monastery at one end of its subway to the ultra-modern underground shopping centre at the other. Between those two points lay countless temples and shrines, several large department stores, dozens of museums and restaurants. Alex found all of it riveting. She could only hope Ben would find her comments on it equally so.

The pure professional, Greg was interested only in speeds and apertures. Out of all the shots he was taking, perhaps a dozen would actually be used in the feature itself, but that in no way deterred him. So far as the magazine was concerned, the main point in his being here at all was to open doors that would not have been open to her had she come alone. Invitations to stay in a Japanese home were few and far between, by all accounts. Almost certainly the Nagasowas would not have been as amenable to a journalistic intrusion without his help.

They ate a late lunch at one of the Yaki restaurants, where they sat around a table with a large centre grill and watched the chef prepare the food. Conversation between the two of them remained stilted—more, acknowledged Alex ruefully, through her own inability to dissemble than any lack of effort on Greg's part.

'How's the article coming along?' he asked on a casual note when they were served.

Alex didn't lift her gaze from her plate. 'Fine, thanks.'

'Care for an objective opinion?'

This time he gained a response in the sharp jerk of her head. 'From you?'

His mouth twisted. 'I'm not in the habit of allowing personal prejudice to cloud my judgement, if that's what you're afraid of. If you're having trouble...'

'Who says I'm having trouble?' she flashed. 'You do your job, Greg, and I'll do mine!'

'You were still at it at one o'clock this morning,' he returned, ignoring the injunction. 'Burning the midnight oil is a sure sign of an uneasy mind. Why don't you leave it alone for a few days?'

'Because I don't work that way,' she said stiffly. 'I like to get down my impressions while they're still fresh, not just rely on notes. If you want to help at all, just try leaving *me* alone!'

His shrug revealed scant sympathy. 'Hardly feasible under the circumstances. We're fellow travellers, darling, like it or not.'

'You know what I mean,' she clipped. 'This morning...' She stopped, biting her lip as the slow smile widened his mouth again.

'As I said, I'm willing to put my finer instincts aside. Especially if it helps settle your mind to your work.' He studied her with malicious amusement as she searched for words with which to squash him. 'Don't bother trying to tell me I'm wrong. I knew you too well not to recognise what you wanted this morning.'

Alex said bitterly, 'You never knew me at all, Greg!'

'I was speaking purely in the physical sense.' His tone hadn't altered. 'In that respect you kept nothing back. I don't mind admitting I found it difficult to turn away from you, but you were right about misusing the bath house. Which leaves bed as a reasonable, and easily managed, alternative. How about tonight?'

'How about cutting out the silly games?' she queried on a tart note. 'You've made your point.'

'Who's playing?' he returned softly.

She made no answer to that. There was little she could say. Given enough encouragement, Greg was capable of carrying this thing through to its conclusion without it meaning a thing to him beyond the immediate satisfaction. It was her own responses that were in doubt. No matter what he'd been in the past, he could still stir her blood, and he knew it. If he decided to take advantage of that fact, she was going to be the only loser.

Yuki had already arrived when they returned to the house in the late afternoon. She greeted them in the hallway, her small, slender body clad in a kimono embroidered with dragons and flowers, her gleaming dark hair piled high and decorated with an ivory comb.

'At home I am traditional Japanese lady,' she acknowledged with a smile when Alex commented admiringly on her appearance. 'It is a form of relaxation for me.' Her glance moved back to Greg, a question in her eyes. 'You have found what you look for?'

'Some of it,' he acknowledged.

'You must keep on looking,' she said cryptically. 'I thought you might be interested to see the *sumo* wrestling this evening?'

'Sounds a good idea,' he agreed. 'Should round off the day nicely.' He was moving as he spoke, not even glancing in Alex's direction. 'I'm for a shower.'

Yuki watched him go, a certain sadness in the dark eyes. 'He is not a happy man,' she said. 'I wish that it could be different.'

She wasn't alone in that, thought Alex painfully. Today had been far from easy, and they still had nine more to get through. She wasn't sure she could take it.

Because it was summer and the evenings warm, the *sumo* bouts were held in an outdoor arena. Although a relatively minor event, this particular *basho* had attracted an audience of hundreds. Yuki had secured seats for the three of them on the very front row before the slightly raised, open platform that constituted the bouting ring.

'From here you will have a good view,' she said.

Almost too good, Alex privately thought when the eight huge *sumotori* who were to compete paraded into the ring. Weighing in at anything between two hundred and three hundred pounds, and wearing nothing but stylised loincloths, many of them looked grossly fat. One in particular, with legs like tree-trunks and a stomach almost as round as he was long, drew cheers and applause from the gathered audience. He was still a very young man, Yuki advised, and set to become one of Japan's élite among wrestlers if he continued the way he had begun.

For Alex, the bouts themselves seemed ridiculously short, the vast majority of the time spent in a ritual of squatting and stamping and face-pulling designed to demoralise the opponent before the actual collision of two great bodies to decide which mass had the greater immovability. Both Greg and Yuki seemed as caught up in the general enthusiasm as anyone else present, discussing the relative merits of each contestant with a knowledge and involvement that left Alex feeling very much the outsider.

'I honestly can't see what all the fuss is about,' she admitted with a certain deliberation during an interval when Greg had gone to fetch drinks from one of the kiosks. 'All that posturing, and for what? Judo calls for so much more skill.'

'*Sumo* was begun two thousand years ago as sacred contests to predict the rice-harvest,' Yuki returned calmly. 'We are great observers of tradition here in Japan. I am sorry that you find it uninteresting, Alex. What will you tell your readers about it?'

Alex was already uncomfortably aware of a lack of courtesy in her assessment. There had been no need to sound quite so disdainful, no matter what her own views. 'I'll tell them what you just told me,' she said, writing it down. 'Tradition I can understand, even if I can't appreciate the spectacle.'

Yuki laughed. 'Greg could teach you a great deal about diplomacy!'

Greg, Alex reflected with feeling, could probably teach a lot of people about a whole lot of things. She let the pause stand for a moment or two before adding on a casual note, 'How long have you two known each other?'

'Since we were children.' The other's tone was reminiscent. 'Our families became close friends. Greg's father was instrumental in persuading my father to allow me to follow an academic career. It was Greg himself who taught me to speak English, while I taught him Japanese. We had many happy times together, he and I.'

Greg was coming back, carrying three plastic cups on a cardboard tray. Alex accepted hers without looking at him, wishing she could teach herself to stop reacting to his closeness. She had to start making some real attempt to pull both herself and her work together. Ben would in no way be impressed by what she had written up to now. It was lacking in all departments.

The atmosphere had grown heavier as the evening progressed, the usual cooling breeze missing. Driving back to Ichijoji in the car they had hired for the duration of their stay in Kyoto, Alex thought that the landscape itself seemed to be brooding.

'We might be in for a summer storm,' Greg advised when she commented on the torpor. 'Feels like it's building up for something. We'll need contingency plans for tomorrow if it rains. Shisendo's strictly a fair-weather place. How about it, Yuki? Something the average tourist wouldn't get to see.'

From the rear seat she had insisted on occupying, the Japanese girl laughed. 'I will put on my thinking cap,' she promised. 'But wherever it is, you must excuse me if I do not accompany you. I have many matters to which I must attend.'

'Pity.' He sounded regretful. 'But understandable when you get home so rarely. Is Tokyo really where you want to spend your life?'

'My work is there,' came the simple answer. 'It is where I must be.'

From her seat at Greg's side, Alex could see out of the corner of her eye the sudden wry twist of his lips. 'Work isn't everything,' he murmured.

'It is for me.' Quietly spoken, the statement carried weight. 'It fills the empty spaces.'

Gazing out through the windscreen along the muted path of radiance cast by the headlights, Alex knew exactly what she meant. Her work had been her lifeline these past two years. All the more reason why she had to make a success of this assignment, because it was all she was going to have in the future, too, unless and until she eventually met someone who could mean as much to her as Greg once had.

On reaching the house she made the excuse of needing to sort out her notes. It was hot in her room. In an effort to catch any vestige of moving air, she slid open the outer screens, standing there for a moment or two to sniff the night scents before getting down to the task in hand. A storm brewing, Greg had said, yet the sky was clear of cloud.

The sound of low voices carried on the stillness, the words themselves indistinguishable by virtue of the fact that they were spoken in Japanese. Greg and Yuki, Alex thought. They appeared to be alone. They had known each other many years, those two. Almost a lifetime, in fact. Yuki must be older than she had first seemed if they had been childhood friends. It seemed strange that she had never married, here in a country where family life was of such importance. Her career had obviously taken first place all along the line.

She could use a little of that same dedication herself right now, Alex acknowledged in sudden determination, turning back into the room. This article wasn't going to write itself.

It was an hour or more before she heard Greg moving around next door. An hour in which she had at last begun to break the deadlock on her creative skills. Re-reading what she had written, she felt her confidence returning a little. It was better—so much better. Closing her mind to outside influences might not be easy, but it certainly paid dividends.

The movement stopped, the silence returning. Alex tried to compose herself for sleep, but her eyelids refused to stay closed. The stillness was uncanny—almost as if the whole world was held in suspended animation. When the low rumble started, she thought at first that it was thunder. Only when the floor beneath her began to shake did she come alive to the reality of what was happening.

The tremor lasted no more than a few seconds, though it seemed an eternity at the time. A faint dust drifted down on her from the ceiling. She lay rigid, waiting for her pulses to stop their mad galloping, for the use to come back to her limbs. She had known, of course, that there was a risk of earthquakes at this time of the year, but had somehow never anticipated experiencing one for herself. She didn't, she thought feelingly, want to experience another!

Movement came from beyond the screen. A moment later Greg slid it back, his very presence a reassurance.

'Are you all right?' he demanded.

'I think so.' Alex forced herself upright, grimacing at the film of dust lying over everything. 'That was scary!'

'Nothing to worry about,' he said. 'I doubt if it registered more than three on the Richter scale.'

'Are there likely to be any more?' she asked, trying to sound as calm and collected about it as he did himself.

'It's possible. They're common enough during the hot season.' He added comfortingly, 'I'm talking about tremors rather than quakes. You'll get used to it. Want a hand shaking out your *futon*?'

'Please.' Alex pushed herself to her feet as he moved across, unsurprised to feel the shakiness in her limbs. 'I suppose the Nagasowas will have taken it all as a matter of course.'

'They'll have assumed I'll be providing any necessary attention, I imagine,' came the dry reply. 'Pointless cleaning up before morning, anyway.'

She took in a careless breath, coughing as the dust caught the back of her throat. The thought of being alone again tonight brought a tremor all her own. She'd never sleep. Not with the possibility of recurrence hanging over her.

'How do they stand it?' she burst out. 'Never knowing when it might happen!'

'Fatalism,' he said. 'Short of leaving this part of the world altogether, there's no other way to look at it. They were born to it, remember.' He smoothed his end of the *futon* and straightened. 'That should do you for the time being.'

'Greg...' his name came out huskily, torn from her without conscious intent '... don't go. Not yet, anyway.'

There was a pause before he turned back slowly to look at her, the expression in his eyes obscured by the darkness. 'If it's a purely platonic comfort you're after, I doubt if I'm capable of providing it.'

'Oh, stop it,' she said wearily. 'What happened was two years ago. Isn't it time we both put it behind us?'

The reply was a moment coming. 'Start afresh, you mean?'

'No, that's not what I mean. Not in the same sense, at least.' She hesitated, not quite sure what exactly it was she wanted to say—only knowing she didn't want to be alone in the darkness. 'Just call a truce, that's all.'

'I don't have a particularly forgiving nature,' he said. 'I'd have thought you'd already realised that. If I stay

with you at all it will be for one reason and one reason
only. It's called compensation. Are you ready to provide
it?'

'No, I'm not!' The moment of weakness had passed,
leaving her quivering with anger and resentment. 'Why
don't you go and ask Yuki, if you're feeling so deprived
of your creature comforts? She may be willing to oblige
an old friend!'

'I told you to leave her name out of it!' His posture,
though unchanged, had stiffened. 'There's never been
anything of that nature between us. There never can be.
If and when she chooses a mate, it will be one of her
own countrymen. She wouldn't have it any other way.'

Alex was motionless, absorbing the clipped statement
with a numbing realisation. So her initial impressions
had not been unfounded after all. Yuki meant far more
to him than just a friend. It explained why he had taken
on this job in the first place. Nothing to do with her. It
had simply provided an excuse to see his real love again.

How long? she wondered dully. Had it happened since
their break-up, or had their whole affair been a sham
from the beginning? He wouldn't be the first man to try
finding solace in another woman when the one he really
wanted was denied him. Nor to keep on looking either,
if it came to that. Not that it was any excuse.

And what of Yuki herself? Was she aware of the way
he felt? Not a happy man, she had said earlier that
evening, which seemed to denote some degree of insight.
Yet her demeanour seemed so natural, so lacking in the
kind of awkwardness one might associate with such
knowledge. On the other hand, who could tell? The
Japanese had a different way of looking at things.

'I'm sorry,' she said haltingly. 'I didn't realise how things were.'

'You still don't.' His tone was short. 'You could no more understand a woman like Yuki than fly!'

'No.' Her throat hurt. 'I don't suppose I could. Does she know?'

'She knows.' He said it without inflection. 'Let's leave it there, shall we?' The pause held deliberation. 'Still want me to stay?'

Alex made a mute gesture in the negative, unable to bring herself to answer. Her head ached with a dull throbbing that threatened to become a real agony. At no time in the whole of their relationship had Greg really felt anything for her. She had simply been an anodyne against the pain of loving and wanting someone he couldn't have. What kind of man was it who could make love so passionately to one woman while feeling emotionally for another?

Any kind, came the bitter answer. Men were adept at separating body from mind.

Although only a few minutes' walk from the city outskirts with its drab apartment blocks and modern villas, Ichijoji was an area of narrow lanes, of steep and isolated paths winding over the forested mountainside, of tiny hidden temples and breathtaking views.

When Greg had been here as a boy the community had been totally rural, Alex gathered over the supper table the following evening. With the rate at which Kyoto was growing, he said, it wouldn't be long before the hedgerows began to disappear and the few remaining rice-fields gave way to the demand for building-land.

'People must have homes in which to live,' declared Yuki, apparently quite prepared to accept the changes in environment. 'Always there are more babies born than there are those who die, so we have a population problem.'

'You could try birth control,' suggested Alex blandly, and drew an unruffled smile.

'So we do, but with so many of us already in being, it is, as you would say, like closing the gate after the horse has left!'

It was Misako who swiftly changed the subject. 'I have managed at last to obtain permission for you to visit the *geisha* house,' she said. 'It must be in the first part of the morning so that you do not interfere too much with the day's routine.'

Greg inclined his head in appreciation. 'That's excellent, Misako! Will tomorrow be all right? We'll be leaving for Shikoku on Monday morning.'

'I am sure tomorrow will be suitable.' She added softly, 'We shall be sad to see you go.' Her glance moved to Alex. 'You will, perhaps, return to Japan one day when there is more time?'

'I doubt if I'll ever have the opportunity,' Alex returned with regretful intonation. 'It's been good of you to let us stay in your home like this.'

'Greg is close to us all,' came the reply. 'Whatever he asks is his.'

Except for the one thing he wanted above all, she thought, avoiding the blue glance from across the table.

The realisation that even in the very beginning of their relationship she had been no more than a substitute for the Japanese girl had gone deep. If she could have disliked her it might have helped a little, only there was nothing to dislike. Telling herself she hated Greg was no solution either.

At least the piece was coming together at last. That was some consolation. Making a good job of this assignment would set her in line for more of the same. Like Yuki herself, she intended making her career the most important thing in her life from now on. It was only deep down inside that she acknowledged the emptiness of that ambition.

Set behind tall iron gates in a quiet backwater of the city, the *geisha* house was reminiscent of a refined girls' school, complete with giggling schoolgirls peeping at the visitors from beneath coyly lowered lids.

They had made the visit early in the morning before classes got under way. As the only male in the vicinity, Greg came in for a lot of attention, which he took in his stride. Permission to photograph carried certain restrictions. Alex left him to his job while she accompanied one of the older pupils on a tour of inspection.

Singing, dancing and playing the *shamisen*—which was rather like a western banjo—were only a few of the accomplishments which went into the training of a *geisha*. In addition she had to be able to converse and create the right atmosphere for her clients, to orchestrate an entire evening's entertainment. The apprenticeship was lengthy, the qualifying examination stringent. Alex doubted if she could have lasted out the first few months, much less whole years of such a strict life-style.

Not that humour was absent. Communication difficulties were overcome by sign language where necessary, laughter never very far away. It was one of the senior pupils called Tomoko, who had a few words of English, who made the suggestion, eyes alight with pure mischief. Urged by the other girls, Alex finally allowed herself to be persuaded. If nothing else, it would be something different to write about.

Looking at the reflection revealed by the long mirror some twenty minutes later, she could scarcely credit her own appearance. Deft fingers had slanted her eyes and whitened her skin with skilfully applied make-up, hiding her hair beneath a black wig already arranged in the traditional upswept style and decorated with jewelled combs. The kimono they had brought her was a thing of beauty in its delicate colours, the *obi* which went about her waist made of pure silk. On her feet she wore *tabi* socks which fastened up the inside of each ankle.

The girls gathered around her were as amused and intrigued by the transformation as she was herself, the laughter and comment needing no translation. Earlier, Greg had requested a shot of the whole 'school' before they left. The notion of including his own colleague in that photograph, unbeknown to him, obviously caught their collective imagination. Alex went along with the idea because it would have seemed churlish to refuse. Greg was sensitive enough to play the game through if he spotted the addition to the group.

They found him in the central courtyard setting up an angled view of the house through an arch of drooping willow. Alex took care to stay in the background as he posed the group on the white stone steps, knowing her eye colour alone would give her away if he got too close. The giggles were getting louder, hands going to mouths. Using the fan she had been given as a shield, Alex joined in. Greg was smiling himself, apparently putting the laughter down to girlish high spirits. She hoped Ben might see fit to use the shot in the feature. He would appreciate the joke.

They had been requested to leave the premises by ten-thirty in order for preparations to be made for a party due to arrive for luncheon at noon: a group of businessmen, Alex had gathered, who would not be amenable to having their relaxation interrupted by journalists of any nationality. By the time she was back in her own clothes, with her face cleansed of all but lipstick and a touch of moisturiser, most of her new friends had melted away, leaving Tomoko to take her to the gates where Greg already waited.

'Get what you wanted?' he asked as they walked to where the car was parked.

'More than I expected,' she acknowledged. 'How about you?'

'Quite a good morning.' He paused to take a quick shot of an old woman hobbling painfully along the pavement. 'I wouldn't mind betting she had her feet bound as a child. Barbaric practice. Thank God it was stopped!' Without looking at her, he tagged on, 'Whose idea was that back there?'

'Tomoko's,' Alex admitted. 'How long did it take you to guess?'

'A few minutes.'

'Considerate of you not to let on.'

'It was too good a joke to spoil.' He paused briefly. 'You made a convincing Japanese.'

'Only on the surface.' Her tone was suddenly brittle. 'I couldn't compete with the real thing.'

'True,' he agreed. 'It's a different culture. You'd have a hard time understanding even a fraction of it.'

'While you have total grasp, I suppose.'

'No,' he said dispassionately. 'Little more than a glimmering. If I spent the whole of my life here I'd still be an outsider. There's no such thing as integration in this country.' He added, 'We'll be leaving Kyoto right after breakfast in the morning, and taking the train down to Iwakuni for the crossing over to Shikoku. That will give us four clear working days before we fly back to Tokyo on Saturday morning. It should be long enough.'

'Why Saturday?' Alex queried, following him to the car. 'Our flight home isn't until Monday.'

'Because there's a lot still to see,' he said.

Yuki would be back in Tokyo by then too, she reflected. No doubt that had some bearing. She knew a growing desire for this job to be over and done with, to be back in familiar surroundings again and free of Greg's presence. It was going to take her a long time to regain the ground she had lost these past days.

CHAPTER FIVE

THE August heat and humidity had reached almost unbearable proportions, although it was still an hour or more before noon. The blast of cooled air as Greg switched on the car ignition was a welcome relief. He let it run for a moment or two before setting off.

'It's too hot to work,' he said. 'I need a long, cool beer. Any objection?'

Alex shook her head. 'I've got enough to be going on with.' She waited until they were moving before tagging on, 'What about Yuki?'

Greg judged a gap between vehicles at the intersection and turned out into the main flow, face revealing little. 'What about her?'

Her shrug was as casual as she could make it. 'I thought she might have arranged something else for this afternoon.'

'This is her vacation,' he said. 'She needs the break. In any case...' He paused there, jaw faintly compressing. 'Let's get out of the city.'

In any case, having her along restricted his pleasure in Yuki's company, Alex concluded. Perhaps initially he had hoped her presence might elicit jealousy on the other's part. Love could make one desperate enough for almost anything, as she knew to her cost. Anyway, it obviously hadn't worked.

They drove out to Kameoka, stopping on the way for a drink and a snack. Greg hired a young man to drive the car back to Arashiyama while they rode the rapids of the Hozu river in a boat trip that took two hours and left Alex feeling very much the worse for wear.

'I'm not really into this white water stuff,' she admitted wryly when they were en route for home again. 'I hope to heaven Ben never decides to feature the Grand Canyon run, or some such!'

'I think he already covered it a few years ago.' Greg was watching the evening traffic. 'You're prepared to go anywhere he might consider sending you?'

'I imagine so.' She slanted a glance at the hard profile. 'It's part of the job.'

'Very different from the fashion world. What changed your outlook?'

'It didn't fulfil me.'

He tilted a lip, but refrained from comment. 'You've only been with *World* six months. I assume there were jobs between?'

'I tried going freelance for a spell,' she acknowledged. 'Interesting, but the income wasn't regular enough.'

'And the man you're going with? What does he do?'

'Minds his own business,' she responded smartly. 'I'm here to mind mine, Greg, not give you a run-down on my private life!'

His shrug was easy. 'Just making conversation. If you'd rather we found some other way of communicating, you only have to say so.'

She ignored the jeer as beneath contempt, yet couldn't deny the pang it elicited. Whether he would really follow through if she gave him the opportunity was open to speculation, but she didn't intend putting him to the test.

She took an hour or so to sort her notes before supper. By tomorrow at this time they would be several hundred miles away, she reflected, taking out the map of Honshu to study the route they would be covering. She would have liked to go to Hokkaido too, but there simply wasn't going to be time. There had to be a limit anyway to how much material she could actually use in the end. That was Ben's pigeon. All she could ask was that he didn't cut out what she considered her best bits.

It was going to seem strange, when she did eventually get back, to lie in a proper bed again. Even the chopsticks had become quite easy to manipulate. No doubt, because of the feature, she would be seeing Greg again over the coming weeks, but it would only be in the confines of the office, not socially. There could never be anything but enmity between them. A thought which brought an ache down deep that wouldn't be shifted.

Yuki had arranged to take them to the *bunraku* theatre for the evening. The performers here were puppets about two-thirds life-size, with articulated limbs and movable facial expressions. Each one was operated on stage by three men dressed from head to foot in black, the first in charge of the body, face and right hand, another working the left hand and the third both legs.

To Alex, the whole thing seemed ludicrous at first. It was only as the play began to evolve that she started to forget about the operators, becoming so wrapped up in the unfolding story, so richly and unmistakably portrayed, that they became an integral part of the scenery. When the play finally ended with a mutual suicide by the two young lovers, she was close to the copious tears being shed by many around her. Whoever it was that had coined the phrase 'oriental inscrutability' had never been to a *bunraku* performance, she concluded.

'That was wonderful!' she exclaimed as they emerged from the theatre. 'I really enjoyed it.'

'Better than the *sumo*?' suggested Yuki with a smile.

'Infinitely!' Greg had gone to fetch the car from its parking place, leaving the two of them to wait. Glancing sideways at the smooth features of her companion, Alex wondered exactly how much she knew of the way things were between her and Greg. She had been the one to arrange the shared accommodation at her parent's home, which suggested that Greg himself must have given the impression that it was what he wanted. Not that it should matter to her, unless she was dog-in-the-manger about him, and she certainly didn't appear to be.

'I'm sorry I was so ungracious the other night,' she added impulsively. 'I was feeling at odds with the whole world!'

'I know that feeling too,' returned the other. 'There are times when my life seems very empty.'

Alex studied her a moment, struck by the underlying sadness in that statement. 'That man, Shige, who was at the flat in Tokyo,' she said on a hesitant note, 'is he . . . special?'

'Just a friend from the university.' The dark eyes held a fleeting pain. 'The man I love is forbidden to me.'

The car was drawing to a stop at the kerbside. Greg leaned across to open both front and rear passenger doors.

'No time for the niceties with this lot piling up on my tail,' he said. 'You'll have to act the feminists for tonight.'

Yuki was smiling again, her momentary lapse already probably regretted. 'We will forgive you, Wilde *san*, just this once!'

Alex slid into the rear seat before anyone could object, leaning back against the leather to try and compose her mind. Just a few simple words, and suddenly everything fell into place. Not just a one-way emotion—nor a new development. Not from the way Yuki had spoken. Greg had to be aware of her feelings, of course. It explained so much about his attitude. Not even close friendship could cut through centuries of inbred exclusion, it seemed. Yuki's own so-called progressiveness was only skin-deep.

She made little contribution to conversation during the drive back to the Nagasowa home. Once or twice she caught Greg's eyes on her through the driving mirror, although he made no comment. They found Haruo in the mood for discussion when they reached the house, the beer already standing by. The way Alex was feeling, it was a relief to leave the two men to it and retire for the night along with Yuki and Misako. There would be time enough for goodbyes to be said in the morning.

She was working on her notes in the early hours when Greg slid the screen between them. He made no attempt to move further into the room, resting a hand on the upper framework as he looked across at her.

'I heard you switch on the light,' he said. 'You're going to be tired in the morning.'

'I couldn't sleep anyway,' Alex admitted, trying to keep her tone level. 'It's too hot.' She paused briefly. 'You don't think we're in for another tremor, do you?'

'Who knows?' He sounded relatively unconcerned. 'If there were any major earth movement in the offing, we'd get some warning from the authorities.' He waited a moment before tagging on, 'What happened between you and Yuki while I was fetching the car?'

Her heart jerked. She said tonelessly. 'Happened?'

'It was obvious something had.'

'Then why not ask her?'

'I'm asking *you*,' he said. 'Yuki keeps her own counsel.'

'An admirable trait. One I might adopt.' She heard the faint unsteadiness in her voice and tried to cover it. 'We talked about the *bunraku* performance, that's all.'

His smile was sardonic. 'Not very plausible. I was watching you in the car. *Bunraku*, I'd have said, was the last thing on your mind.'

'You should have kept your eyes on the road,' she retorted. 'Now, if you don't mind, I have work to do.'

A spark lit the blue eyes. 'Nothing that can't wait.'

'My editor wouldn't agree with you. Neither,' she added hardily, 'would I. My job is important to me.'

He moved with surprising speed as she put pen to paper again, yanking both items from her hands and tossing them aside. 'I asked you a question!'

Anger flared in her, fed by all the pent-up anguish of the past two years. She came to her feet to face him, eyes blazing contempt. 'Afraid I told her just what kind of man you are?' she flung at him. 'Is that it? I wouldn't disillusion her that far!'

His eyes were narrowed dangerously. 'And what kind of man am I?'

'A cheat and a liar will do for starters,' she flashed, losing what restraint she had left in a sudden rush of blood to the head. 'Samantha Price wasn't the first, was she, Greg? Any more than she'd have been the last!'

The sudden blanking out of all expression was more curbing than any amount of invective. He was looking at her as if he'd never seen her before.

'What the devil are you talking about?' he demanded. 'There was never anything between Samantha and me.'

He was so convincing, she thought bitterly. So much the injured party! Only, no amount of denial on his part could alter the truth of the matter. It would be a relief in so many ways to have it out in the open at last.

'I'd hardly expect you to admit it,' she retorted. 'You couldn't be honest with me then; why start now? I suspected what was going on before I went to Paris, of course. What I lacked was proof.'

There was no flicker in the hard regard. 'I gather you found it?'

'I had it pushed under my nose! The evening I spoke to you on the phone wasn't the first time I'd rung. The night before it was Samantha who answered.'

He continued to study her, expression controlled. 'And?'

She stared at him, nonplussed for a moment, then rallied again. 'You were together, *you* tell *me*. Careless of you to let her answer the phone at all, I'd have thought.'

'It might have been,' he said, 'if I'd been there at the time.'

Her laugh grated. 'You're trying to tell me she was in the flat on her own? Then she must have had a key.'

'I'm telling you,' he said on the same flat, unemotional note, 'that I wasn't around when that call came through. From what I remember of that evening, I'd run into Samantha—and the man she's since married— in town, and brought them both back to the flat for a drink while I changed before going out with them to dinner. A habit of mine, if you recollect. If she spoke to you that night it was probably while I was in the shower.'

The silence in the room seemed to deepen in direct proportion to the seconds ticking by. Gazing into taut features, Alex made a supreme effort to gather herself together. 'And I'm supposed to believe she never even mentioned the call to you?'

'No, she didn't. That I'd certainly have remembered.' He paused, mouth grim. 'What exactly did you say to her?'

Alex swallowed on the sudden hard obstruction in her throat. She felt as if the ground were being slowly pulled from beneath her feet. 'I...well...nothing. What should I have said?'

'Something like "What are you doing there?" might have been a start. If you simply broke the connection, she probably assumed it was a wrong number, so there was no point in mentioning it.' He waited, lifting an interrogative brow when she failed to respond. 'Was that the whole basis of your...proof?'

Her chin tilted. 'No, it wasn't! I found her tissue case in my make-up drawer—complete with initial. It didn't walk there on its own!'

'I imagine not,' he said. 'I don't recall every detail of that evening, but there's every chance I offered Sam the use of the bedroom to check her appearance before we left. She was always the perfectionist when it came to the way she looked. Not a hair out of place, or a shine where it shouldn't be. A nice girl, and a superb subject. She was never any more than that. Whatever else you saw, or thought you saw, was all in your own mind!'

Not a chance! she thought. For a brief moment there he had almost convinced her, but the whole explanation was just too pat. His mind was sharp. It always had been.

'Good, but not quite good enough,' she said scornfully. 'I'm not a fool, Greg. You'd been seeing her for weeks before that! Your whole attitude towards me had altered.'

The skin was drawn over hard male cheekbones, his mouth a thin, tight line. 'You're probably right there. I'd begun losing hope that you were ever going to develop some real depth of feeling where we were concerned. All you seemed to want was an on-going affair. No commitment.'

Breath caught suddenly in her throat, she said haltingly, 'I . . . thought that was what *you* wanted.'

'Then you were wrong. All right, I asked you to move in with me. It's what's called putting the cart before the horse.' There was no humour in his voice. 'I wanted you with me, but I didn't think you were ready then to make any permanent decision. You were in love with the idea of being in love. Marriage needs more than that if it's going to last. I planned on working up to it.'

Alex's head was spinning. She had to force the words out. 'What about Yuki? Wasn't she the one you loved?'

'Still is,' he responded hardily. 'You don't stop loving someone just because you can't have them. Neither was I going to spend the rest of my life in a monastery. The way I felt about you didn't come under the same heading, but it could have been just as good, given the opportunity to mature.'

'I don't believe it,' she said desperately. 'You're just saying it!'

His shrug suggested indifference. 'Why should I lie about it? It doesn't gain me anything. I loved an image I had of a girl who didn't exist. I don't suppose I'm the first to do that. Anyway, it's all in the past, as you keep telling me. Whatever it was I felt, you killed it stone-dead the day you wrote that letter. Few men could take that kind of rejection in their stride.' He paused, mouth taking on an added slant. 'I suppose I should be grateful for learning the truth at last. Good for the ego, if nothing else.'

She said painfully, 'If there's any truth at all in what you've just said, why did you bothering coming on this trip when you found out who you were going to be travelling with? You don't need the money. That was just an excuse.'

'Oddly enough, I rather fancied the job itself. You were a complication I'd as soon have done without, but I was dammed if I was going to step down because of it.' He studied her, registering the look slowly surfacing in her eyes with sardonic expression. 'Finally getting through, is it?'

'Greg, I'm . . . sorry.' It sounded lame even to her own ears. She felt numbed through; unable to cope with it all. She could hardly bring herself to look at him. 'What else can I say?'

'Not a lot,' he agreed. 'You already said it.' He drew in a sudden harsh breath, as if the memory alone was a knife twist. 'You ruined everything we might have had because you didn't have the guts to face me with it! Do you have any idea at all what you put me through two years ago?'

'No more than I went through myself,' she defended, and saw his mouth curl.

'I doubt that.'

'I loved you,' she protested huskily. 'I was hurt, and I wanted to hurt back.'

'You mean your pride took a knock. You wouldn't know love if it hit you in the face!'

The sudden hot rage was as much a self-defence as righteous anger. 'Oh, and you're such an expert, of course! Off with the old love and on with the new! All right, so maybe, just maybe, I was wrong about Samantha, but I'd be willing to bet there were others. You were only interested in one thing!'

'Is that a fact?' He spoke with a clipped quietness that contracted her stomach muscles in sudden apprehension. 'In which case, I may as well live up to expectations.'

He was moving as he spoke, hooking a foot behind her ankle to send her crashing on to her back on the *futon*. Alex put up both hands in a futile gesture of defence as he followed her down, only to have her wrists seized in an iron-hard grip and forced back over her head.

Something inside her froze the cry before it could break from her lips. She fought him silently, viciously, as he took both wrists in the one hand and used the other to tear open her robe. Only when she felt the touch of his fingers against her bare flesh did she stop struggling, her breath coming in shuddering gasps.

'Greg...don't!' she pleaded.

The face above her had a devilish cast. 'Shut up,' he gritted. 'You owe me this!'

She closed her eyes as he dropped his head to find her breast with his lips, her senses leaping to the exquisite sensation. It had been so long, so very, very long. She had almost forgotten how it felt! It was impossible to control the response spiralling upwards from that central core. She could feel herself melting, beginning to move against him, the past receding with each fluttering heartbeat until there was nothing in her mind but the moment.

Sensing the change in her, he relaxed his grip on her wrists to strip off the *yukata*. She saw his jaw contract as he looked at her, and knew a flooding of relief that her body could still bring that look to his eyes. She couldn't wait for him to slide out of his own robe, pushing it back over broad shoulders to run her fingers over hard muscle with deep-throated murmurs of pleasure, the memories spilling into each other, cancelling out time. They were together again. Nothing else mattered but that. Together again!

He held away from her for a moment, but only to remove the robe altogether, coming down over her again to fit his body to hers in the way she remembered so well. His mouth was passionate, demanding, rousing her to fever-pitch. She trembled uncontrollably in his embrace as he traced a passage down the full length of her body to deliver that most intimate of kisses, writhing in his grasp as moan after moan was wrung from her lips.

Then he was coming back to her, sliding between pliant thighs to fill the emptiness of those years, moving inside her with strength and purpose until all consciousness converged on that single driving force, and she was lost...

She awoke to daylight, lying there for a long moment gazing at the ceiling while her mind explored the events of the night—feeling her body stir afresh at the memories evoked. They had fallen asleep in each other's arms, just as they used to. Once during the night she had opened her eyes to see the dark head close beside her, and had gone back to sleep secure in the knowledge of Greg's presence. He wasn't there now, of course. He wouldn't be, would he? Last night had been the product of emotions far removed from love.

Her own feelings this morning were confused to say the least. She wanted him, yes, but the doubts still remained. Two years of mistrust didn't disappear completely overnight, no matter what the incentive. How Greg himself was likely to react she couldn't begin to guess. He was in so many ways a stranger to her. Even if it were really true that he had planned on asking her to marry him at some point, it hadn't been for the reasons she would have wanted. Although, if she had never known about Yuki, would she have ever realised the difference? came the thought, dismissed with a mental shrug. It didn't have any bearing, did it? That was then and this was now. There was no going back.

She was about to stir herself into some kind of action when the screen was slid back. Greg was already fully dressed apart from his shoes. Alex came up on an elbow, feeling her face flush as she met the blue eyes. He looked so totally unaffected by what had passed between them— not even mocking her obvious discomfiture.

'We're going to miss our train if you don't get a move on,' he said. 'The last thing I want is a rushed departure.'

Especially when it came to saying goodbye to Yuki, Alex thought fleetingly, and felt her heart contract.

'I was just coming,' she acknowledged, only too aware of her nudity beneath the thin covering of the *yukata* thrown over her. Greg must have covered her, she realised. At which point she wasn't certain. Not that it mattered, anyway. There was a great difference between

last night and this morning. She didn't possess the kind
of nerve it would take to reveal herself to him in cold
blood, so to speak.

As if recognising her dilemma, he turned to go, still
without expression of any nature. His name came to her
lips involuntarily.

'Greg...'

His head swivelled towards her again. 'Greg...what?'
he asked on a cool note.

She made a small, helpless gesture. 'I'd have thought
that obvious. We can't just ignore what happened.'

'On the contrary, I thoroughly enjoyed it. I rather
gathered you did, too.'

She said slowly, 'There has to be more to it than that.'

'Why?' he demanded. 'Did you think that was all it
was going to take to cancel out the whole affair?'

His choice of words made her wince. 'That's not what
I meant, and you know it!'

'Do I?' He studied her, for the first time allowing the
contempt to show. 'All I know is you didn't lose your
talent for giving a man a good time. In fact, I'd say
you'd even learned a thing or two since the last time we
got it together.'

'That's not true!' She came bolt upright, oblivious
now of her nudity, eyes darkened by pain. 'There hasn't
been anyone else. Not in that sense!'

He shrugged. 'I'll take your word for it. Don't spend
too long in the bath house.'

She remained where she was for a long, numb moment
after he had gone from the room. No quarter to be given,
was it? Pride came to her rescue, stiffening her backbone
both literally and metaphorically. If that was the way he
wanted it, so be it. Two could play the same game.

*   *   *

Crossing the Inland Sea was an experience Alex would not have missed. Pine-covered islands lay scattered across the calm blue waters beneath a sky hazed with heat, some no more than a fist of rock, others occupied by fishing communities, most untouched by the industrial clutter that despoiled so much of the mainland.

'Part of Shikoku's west coast has been built up,' Greg advised, leaning on the ferry rail at her side, 'but where we're going you'll find it more or less as it was a hundred years ago. How good a swimmer are you?'

'Fair,' she acknowledged.

'Can you dive at all without scuba gear?'

'I've done a little.' She glanced at him swiftly, still fighting shy of meeting the blue eyes head on. 'Am I going to be doing any diving?'

'If you want to see real pearl fishing as well as the commercialised kind,' he said. 'There's a village on the west coast where they still collect from natural oyster beds. I went down with them last year.'

'With an underwater camera?'

'Yes. I can dig out the negatives if Ben wants to take a look. I suppose you could use them yourself if the idea doesn't appeal.'

'What I can't see or experience for myself, I don't write about,' she declared. 'Are we going to be staying in the village itself?'

'That's the idea.' He straightened up from the rail. 'I'm for a cold beer. Interested?'

Alex shook her head. 'I'll stay here. The view's too good to miss.'

She watched him walk away, a tall, clean-limbed figure of a man in the casual white trousers and black shirt. He had been casual himself these past hours—almost as if nothing at all existed between them. Whatever he had said to Yuki before leaving this morning, it had been said in private. Neither of them had shown any emotion when the moment of goodbye came. No matter how she tried, she couldn't understand the other's attitude. If her love for Greg was as great as she had intimated, then surely the sacrifice of an ideal was a small price to pay?

But then, *she* wasn't Japanese, she reminded herself wryly. How could she say what was or wasn't vital to these people?

Her own emotions were still in turmoil. If Greg was telling the truth with regard to Samantha, then she was guilty of allowing circumstantial evidence and so-called women's intuition to ruin a relationship that had meant more to her than anything in the world at that time. No, not *anything*, she acknowledged in a sudden burst of wry self-judgement. Her pride had obviously been more important to her at the time. Getting through this next week was not going to be easy, but it had to be done. At least with everything in the open now there would be no more undercurrents to contend with. Once back in England, they could each of them go their own way again without heartache.

Liar, she thought depressedly. The heartache would be with her for a long time to come.

They lingered in Matsuyama only as long as it took to hire a car. Alex would have liked to have taken the cableway up the forested hill at the city centre to look at the castle that crowned its summit, but Greg wanted to make their destination before nightfall.

'You can see it on the way back,' he said. 'We're taking an early flight to Tokyo on Saturday, so we'll need to be here overnight Friday.'

Four full days. And in what circumstances? They were going to a small, probably almost primitive village. Conditions were hardly going to be ideal. On the other hand, Greg obviously no more wanted to be in close confines with her again than she with him. He knew these people. It was up to him to sort it out.

It was probably mental rather than physical exhaustion that finally claimed her. When she opened her eyes again the urban landscape had given way to some of the most beautiful coastal scenery she had ever seen, with magnificent views out over the Inland Sea.

'Sadamisaki Peninsula,' supplied Greg as she sat up straighter in her seat. 'We're almost there.'

The setting sun was shining almost directly into their eyes. Greg had pulled down his visor. Alex did the same. 'How long was I asleep?' she asked. 'It seemed I'd only just shut my eyes.'

'A couple of hours,' he said. 'Hardly surprising. It's been a very full day.'

And an even fuller night, she thought cynically. At least tonight she could look forward to a good sound sleep. From what Greg had told her of his plans for their stay, she was going to need it.

CHAPTER SIX

THE tiny community of Usukimiya lay contained within a small bay, its traditional wooden houses thatched with dried grasses and companionably grouped. Work was finishing for the day as they arrived, men and women alike joining forces to pull the boats up the fine white beach. Greg was greeted like an old friend, the smiles and exclamations cutting across language barriers to include Alex herself in the welcome.

The house in which they were apparently to stay was a little larger than its neighbours in that it possessed two rooms in addition to its tiny kitchen and covered terrace. It belonged to an elderly man Greg addressed as Tsugi *san* who proudly indicated that one whole room was to be theirs.

Alex held her tongue with an effort until they were alone together in the restricted area, facing up to him with determination in her eyes and voice.

'You'd better get this sorted out, hadn't you? I'm not sharing a room with you, Greg. I wouldn't share a pigsty with you!'

'They don't keep pigs here,' he came back imperturbably. 'A few cows, maybe, up top. Much of their diet consists of fish and poultry. The protein keeps them going.'

'I didn't ask for an environmental run-down,' she snapped. 'Just do something about it!'

He spread his hands. 'There isn't a lot I can do. This is the only accommodation available. What's the difference? We've been sharing since we got here.'

'Not like this!' with a disparaging gesture.

'This is how the other half lives,' he said drily. 'It was the contrasts you wanted, wasn't it?'

She bit her lip, already ashamed of the fleeting contempt. It wouldn't have bothered her normally where or how she stayed, but this situation was something else. The room was tiny, the walls themselves almost within touching distance. Two *futons* would take up most of the available floor space.

'I'll sleep outside if necessary,' she clipped. 'It's warm enough.'

Greg shook his head. 'No, you won't. That would be taken as a gesture of dissatisfaction. The Japanese may be great at self-disparagement but they don't expect it from foreigners. We'll make the best of it we can. You don't have to like it.'

'Did you plan this?' Alex demanded fiercely. 'Is this your way of getting back at me for that letter?'

'I already got back at you for that letter,' he said, registering the sudden increase of colour in her face with cynical amusement.' The pause was calculated. 'Not that I'm saying I'd turn my back on you if you happened to feel like offering the same again.'

She stiffened. 'Hardly likely!'

'Pity.' He sounded anything but regretful. 'So we'll just agree to suffer through it, shall we?'

There was no answer to that. He obviously didn't expect one. Turning away, he squatted to unfasten his bag, leaving Alex to force herself into movement. As he said, they were going to have to make the best of it. Only let him come near her again and she wouldn't care who knew their circumstances!

There was no bathroom as such, just a basic water-closet outside: the villagers themselves shared a communal bathhouse. Hot water was brought to them by Tsugi's two daughters, together with clean *yukatas*. Greg stripped off his outer wear without hesitation as soon as the two giggling girls had gone.

'You can close your eyes if you want to,' he taunted.

It was absolutely ridiculous, Alex acknowledged, that she should feel any constraint with a man in whose arms she had lain naked and unashamed. His back was turned to her, tanned and muscular. An inner part of her yearned to slide her arms around his waist and press her lips to the smooth warm skin; the other half shied away from any kind of contact at all. Four days of this was going to be more than she could stand!

'Are we here right through till Friday?' she asked, slowly unbuttoning her cotton shirt.

He answered without turning his head. 'Only the two nights. Wednesday, we go to Uwajima for the sea farms and the bullfights.'

'I hate bullfighting!' she stated.

'These aren't like the Spanish variety. Anyway,' he added hardily, 'that's where *I'm* heading. You please yourself.'

With only the one vehicle, she had little choice, she fumed. She needed him, she knew that. The job aside, she had no wish to find herself stranded in a part of the country where she couldn't even make herself understood.

Greg left her to it as soon as he was clad. Washed, and wearing the remaining *yukata*, she went to join the family in the other room. This one was larger, and contained the usual low table. A niche in one wall held an arrangement of dried grasses and driftwood, with a single lotus flower as a focal point. Artistic appreciation was obviously not confined just to the upper classes in this country, Alex conceded.

There was a son in addition to the two daughters. Together with the mother, a self-effacing personage who emerged only at brief intervals from the minute kitchen premises, they made quite a crowd.

Fish of several kinds formed the basis of the evening meal. Seated on one of the thin cushions called *zabuton*, Alex tried to follow the general conversation, but even with Greg to act as interpreter there was little more she could do than nod and smile.

Dreading the appearance of the beer that had usually signalled Haruo's intention of prolonging the discourse, she was heartily relieved when an early retirement was indicated. These people began work again at first light, Greg advised. Unlike the culture farms further down the coast, many oysters had to be brought to the surface and opened before a pearl would be found, and only certain ones selected in the first place.

'I'm going for a breather along the shore,' he announced when they were back in their room again. 'Do you want to come?'

Even with all the screens open to catch the evening breeze, it had been hot and sticky indoors. The invitation had not been extended with any great enthusiasm, but anything had to be better than waiting here alone for his return, she thought. At least outside there was room to move. With the two *futons* laid, there was only just space enough between to walk.

They donned their own footwear for the venture, but retained the *yukatas*.

'I must get myself one of these to take home,' Alex remarked as they moved across the white sand. 'They're marvellous for relaxing in!' She turned her face towards the sea, drawing in a deep breath. 'Ozone smells the same the world over, doesn't it? We could be in Devon or Cornwall right now.'

'Not in this heat.' Greg turned to look back at the already darkened village tucked into the inner curve of the little bay. 'Peaceful, isn't it? I often think of this place when I'm feeling fed up with city life.'

She said softly, 'Did you ever consider coming back to Japan on a permanent basis?'

'On occasion,' he acknowledged. 'Not lately.'

'Because of Yuki?'

His face closed up again. 'I don't want to talk about Yuki.'

'Not to me, you mean?'

'If you like.'

He moved on, hair lifting to the sultry breath of wind. Alex followed him resignedly, aware of ruining the brief moment of peace between them. This was hopeless, she thought. They had to find some level at which they could communicate.

'Can't we agree to put it aside just for the duration of this trip?' she asked the unrelenting back. 'I realise how you feel, but...'

'I doubt it.' His voice had an edge still. 'I'm not all that sure myself.' He slowed again, turning his head to look at her as she came alongside. There was no moon, but the stars were bright enough to outline his features quite clearly. 'You knocked me for six last night. In all these months it never once occurred to me to question your motives in leaving. I'm not going to repeat the denials. That's water under the bridge, anyway. What I'd like to know is why the devil you didn't face me with it at the time?'

Alex swallowed painfully on the lump in her throat. 'You said it yourself. Pride. If it's any consolation, I regretted that letter more than I ever regretted anything before—or since. It was . . . unnecessary.'

His smile was faint. 'That's one way of putting it. You use words as weapons, Alex. You always did. If there's one thing the male ego can't take it's contempt from a woman. I could have throttled you when I saw you in the office that day.'

Her voice sounded rough. 'But you got over it.'

'Yes, I got over it.' There was a pause, a sudden change of tone, as if he already regretted the momentary lapse. 'Problem is I'm finding it difficult to turn off the switch you pulled last night. You were more than . . . accommodating.'

Warmth seared her skin. 'You didn't give me much opportunity to be anything else!'

He laughed. 'I didn't give you much opportunity to escape justice, maybe. The kind of response I got was beyond all expectations!' He shot out a staying hand as she started to move blindly away. 'Don't go. Isn't that what you said to me the other night?'

Alex resisted the urge to shake the hand from her shoulder with an effort. If there had been any remission at all in his attitude a moment ago, it was no longer apparent. If he was as innocent as he made out in this affair, then the whole of the blame for their break-up lay with her, but that didn't mean she had to take any-thing he cared to dish out by way of a penance.

'The earth isn't likely to start shaking tonight,' she said frigidly, and saw his mouth tilt.

'Don't count on it!'

Her breath came out on a long drawn sigh. She said with feeling, 'Greg, this is ridiculous! Why can't we just forgive and forget? Last night was a mistake—on both our parts. Don't try to compound it.'

'I'll think about it,' he said. 'Only some urges don't fade for the telling.'

'Then go and jump in the sea!' she snapped.

This time she pulled free, but she didn't get very far. He seized her from behind, spinning her round to hold her with both hands hard on her upper arms as he looked down into her angry face.

'Don't walk away from me,' he said softly. 'Not before I'm through with you.'

She quivered when he found her mouth, fighting to stay aloof from that searching, searing kiss. It was all the more difficult because she hadn't anticipated this de-velopment when he invited her to accompany him; she wasn't prepared. If he had planned it this way then he had put on a very good act back there of uninterest. Not that it helped at all now.

One hand slid inside her robe, covering her breast. His thumb caressed roughly, springing her nipple erect and drawing a smothered sound of protest from her throat.

'Put your hands on me,' he demanded on a low, sud-denly gruff note. 'I want to feel your hands on me, Alex!'

Without a will of her own, she placed both palms flat on his chest where the robe had come open, spreading her fingers through the wiry whorls of hair to follow them with her lips the way she used to do so long, long ago; tasting the salt on his skin, breathing in the male scent of him, feeling her senses coming alive again.

Sanity returned like a dash of cold water in the face as he lifted her away from him. He was breathing a little faster himself, but still in control, expression derisive.

'Enough for now, I think. The rest can wait *my* pleasure.'

Standing there gazing at him, Alex felt a shudder run the length of her spine. She had done this to him. The old Greg would never have stooped to such gambits.

'What good is this kind of thing going to do?' she queried on a shaky note. 'You're just being vindictive!'

'That's right. And enjoying it.' There was no softening of expression. 'We've two years to make up for— and a bare week to do it in. You're going to remember this trip for a long time to come, Alex. I'll make sure of it!'

There was no point in reasoning with him. Not right now, at any rate. She turned away from him and began to walk back along the beach the way they had come, trying not to stumble in the soft sand. Because of the latter she couldn't be sure whether he was following her, but she didn't look back. Both body and mind felt bruised. He wasn't going to forgive. Not in a thousand years! She'd been foolish to fancy that he might.

The little room seemed even smaller and darker than before. Alex crept in through the outer screen, afraid of awakening the sleeping family on the other side of the thin partition. She was going to be safe enough from Greg's vindictiveness in here at least, unless he wanted to run the risk of losing face with his host. Before the next opportunity arose, she had to find a way of reaching through this tough, hard shell of his and find the inner man again.

Several minutes passed before he came quietly through the screen. Alex was already lying under the cover, although she knew she wouldn't be able to stand the heat for long. He didn't say a word, letting himself down on to the other mattress to lie with hands clasped behind his head and eyes on the ceiling. He was still in the same position when she finally fell asleep.

The reefs on which the villagers were working lay half a mile from shore. Each small, sail-driven boat was shared by a couple—usually male and female—who took it in turns to do the diving. Past the age of doing any pearl-seeking himself, Tsugi insisted on taking the visitors out to the worksite in his own boat, settling down under a canvas shelter rigged in the stern to wait with apparent contentment until they conveyed a wish to return to shore.

Crucial to the life of the village though the industry was, there was no shortage of laughter and enjoyment. The discovery half-way through the morning of one small but otherwise perfect pearl brought jubilation. The entire population could live for a week on the proceeds from such a find.

Greg managed to bring up some samples of his own, none of which proved productive. Lacking the lung capacity to stay down even a third of the time managed by most, Alex contented herself with viewing only, entranced by the colours of the reef, the variety of plant and sea-life, the sheer beauty of this underwater world. There was so much she wanted to say about Usukimiya, yet it would have to be compressed into a few short paragraphs. One day, she thought half whimsically, she would like to write travel books for a living.

Consisting mostly of fruit, lunch was eaten on site. Afterwards there was a half-hour resting period before work began again. Tsugi had fallen asleep in his corner, snoring softly. Sprawled across the bottom of the boat with head comfortably supported on the gunwhale, Greg showed no immediate inclination to move.

'Not a bad life,' he murmured. 'Pity it can't last.'

'Is that a certainty?' asked Alex.

His shoulders lifted. 'Tsugi admitted last night that more of the younger ones are leaving to look for work in the cities. There's going to come a time when there aren't enough people left to make it pay at all.'

'What will happen to the village then?'

'Those still capable might get work at one of the sea farms. The rest will probably turn to fishing for a living.' He turned his head to look at her, catching her in the very act of appraising the strong clean lines of his near-naked body. 'A pity,' he added softly, 'we aren't alone. I'm having difficulty keeping my mind on the job too. That bikini of yours covers just enough to whet the imagination!'

'That wasn't the intention,' she responded frostily. 'It just happens to be the only one I have with me. If I'd realised we'd be doing this kind of thing, I'd have brought a full suit.'

'And robbed the fish of an eyeful? Shame.' He lifted an unanticipated hand to trace a bead of perspiration running down between her breasts, smiling at her involuntary tremor. 'You're overheated. Too much sun, maybe?'

She jerked away from the questing finger, not sufficiently in command of herself to manage an equable answer. She wanted him so badly, it was an ache deep inside her. If only she could resurrect the old Greg. Just to see him smile at her again without mockery would be something. Only it wasn't likely, was it? The old Greg was gone for good. He might be intent on giving her a bad time now, but once they were back in England she doubted if they would be seeing much, if anything, of each other again.

'Don't back off,' he said. 'You're in no danger with Sleeping Beauty there likely to open his eyes at the crucial moment—much as I'd like to indulge the two of us. Not that a small boat is the ideal venue anyway. How about the beach tonight? Did you ever make love on warm sand with the waves lapping your ankles?'

From somewhere Alex found the necessary control, switching on a derisive little smile of her own. 'No, but obviously you did.'

'All it needs is imagination,' he returned imperturbably. 'I can see you now, stretched out in the moonlight, your hair spread in a fan round your head—the way it was the other night. I'd like to photograph you that way. Temptation, I'd call it. Or downfall. I'm not sure which.'

'Shut up!' She almost hissed the words, her whole body tensed in angry repudiation. 'You're not in the least bit funny!'

Dark brows lifted. 'Who's laughing? It has to happen again somewhere. We're neither of us going to get through the rest of this trip without some degree of satisfaction.'

Alex stood up with a jerk that rocked the boat, resisting with an effort the urge to kick him in the ribs. 'I'm going down again. I prefer the atmosphere!'

She went in cleanly, kicking downwards with all her strength. The water was translucent at this depth, the coral below her descending gently at first before sheering off into depths the sunlight couldn't reach. Sea anemones waved enticing fronds at passing fish. Alex had long given up trying to count the different varieties of marine life. Naming even a small percentage would be difficult enough.

The sudden burning pain across the back of her thigh constricted her lungs. Panicking, she began clawing her way upwards again, driving herself against the spreading ache in her chest. Her leg felt on fire, the muscles drained of use. Above, she could see sunlight sparkling the surface. Too far, that part of her mind still capable of rational thought assessed.

The last of her breath was gone, the pain in her chest a growing agony. On the very edge of unconsciousness, she was aware of some change in the pressure in her ears, felt a body brush hers and two hands grip her tightly about the waist, drawing her upwards. Then she was breaking surface, gasping in breaths of precious, glorious air, tears of mingled pain and relief running down her cheeks to join the salt already there.

Greg kept a tight hold on her until they reached the boat. Tsugi was there to help her back on board, the words of concerned commiseration needing no translation. Hauling himself over the side behind her, Greg sat for a brief moment to steady his own breathing before moving to where she lay huddled.

'You forgot to hyperventilate,' he said. 'For God's sake, Alex, you've been doing it all morning!'

'Something stung me,' she got out between clenched teeth. 'It hurts like fury!'

His expression altered. 'Where?'

Moving at all was painful. She heard the breath hiss between his teeth as he looked at the red swelling on her thigh. 'Sea anemone,' he said. 'I warned you not to go near them.'

'I didn't think I had.' She was shivering despite the heat. 'I think,' she added faintly, 'I'm going to be sick.'

It was Greg who held her head while she leaned over the side of the boat, Greg who cradled her in his arms during the journey back to shore, Greg who carried her, unprotesting, up to the house to lay her down on the *futon* Tsugi made haste to unfold.

A bowl of clean, warm water was brought, together with cloths and some kind of salve. Alex lay on her face, while Greg gently bathed the swollen and throbbing area, swallowing on the nausea that kept coming over her still. She felt drained of all energy, her limbs like lead weights. Whatever the poison contained within the anemone's fronds, it had to be virulent to cause this much reaction.

'Nobody ever pinned the exact toxin down,' Greg acknowledged when she murmured the question. 'That's why there's no antidote. It's going to take twenty-four hours or so to work through your system, but the pain should start to decrease quite soon.' He was applying salve as he spoke, his touch so gentle it was soothing in itself. 'Better get out of these things and into a *yukata*.'

She felt so utterly lifeless that he had to help her out of the bikini, but she was past caring. He was wearing nothing but trunks himself, the hair on his chest silvered with dried salt. She would have given anything at that moment just to be held again in his arms, not in passion but in simple comfort. It was on the tip of her tongue to make the plea, but he was already getting to his feet.

'I'll look in again in an hour or so,' he said. 'Try and get some sleep. That's the best antidote.'

For what? Alex asked herself heavily as he turned away. The poison in her system was only a part of her malady.

Surprisingly enough, she did sleep eventually, awakening again to find the pain dulled to a distant throbbing. The weakness and nausea, however, were still with her. Even lifting her head from the small, hard pillow was an effort.

Tomorrow they were supposed to be leaving for Uwajima, she recalled. They had only three days left before returning to Tokyo, five before leaving for home. She didn't want to go back. Not the way things were. Yet they seemed as far away as ever from reaching any kind of understanding. Greg had always loved Yuki, that was a fact she had to accept. She had never been more than second best. All the same, she still loved and wanted him. More than she had ever wanted anyone or anything in her life. Somehow she had to get that through to him.

As if in answer to her thoughts, the subject of them came into the room, dropping to his knees at her side to put a cool hand to her forehead.

'How do you feel?' he asked.

'Better than I did,' she acknowledged. 'Just so dreadfully weak.'

His nod was reassuring. 'No more than can be expected. By this time tomorrow you should be OK again.'

'But we're supposed to be going to Uwajima,' she murmured. 'There's such a lot we still have to cover!'

'What doesn't get seen gets left,' he stated firmly. 'We don't leave here until you're fit to travel. In the meantime, you shouldn't waste your strength talking.'

'I want to talk,' she responded, throwing caution aside. 'It might be the only chance I get.'

He sat back on his heels to look at her, the expression in his eyes faintly quizzical. 'About what?'

Alex swallowed on the dryness in her throat. 'Us. How much longer do I have to go on paying for the mistakes I've made, Greg?'

It was a moment before he replied, mouth slanted a little. 'Consider the debt settled as of now.'

'Does that mean you've forgiven me?'

'Does that mean you believe my side of it?' he countered.

'Yes,' she said. 'Yes, it does.' She drew in a long breath and let it out again. 'I really messed things up, didn't I?'

He shrugged, his face giving little away. 'It's in the past. Maybe it's better we leave it there.'

She forced herself to say it. 'What about the present?'

There was no change of expression. 'What would you like me to tell you?'

'The way you . . . feel.'

His smile had a cynical edge. 'I thought I'd made that pretty obvious.'

'I don't mean just physically.' She swallowed again, driving herself on. 'You said the other night that what you felt for me could have been as good in its way as what you felt for Yuki. Was that true too?'

'I'd say so.' He sounded quite unemotional about it. 'There are different kinds of love. And if you're trying to ask me could I feel that same way again, the answer is no. Are you hungry at all?'

Alex shook her head, not trusting her voice. She had asked and been told: there was no going back. At least she knew now where they stood. Learning to live with that knowledge was something else again.

CHAPTER SEVEN

THEY left Usukimiya on the Thursday morning after a day and night which for Alex at least had dragged interminably. She had felt well enough to travel by early afternoon, and had said so, but Greg had refused to budge. Thirty-six hours' rest was essential in order to make sure all the toxin had been cleared from her bloodstream, he had declared. They would make up the lost time one way or another.

His attitude this morning was difficult to pin down. Relaxed enough on the surface, yet with an element of withdrawal about him too. Only he need have no fear, Alex told herself heavily. She had no intention of repeating her overture. He had made his feelings—or lack of them—only too clear.

'Glad to be heading back to the modern world again?' he asked as they drove back along the peninsula.

'Depends what you mean by modern,' she returned. 'I'll be glad to be home again. It seems ages since we left England.'

'Ten days,' on a dry note. 'Not exactly a lifetime. All part of the job, wasn't that what you said the other day? Providing Ben Reynolds likes what you do with the material, it will all have been worth while.'

Not all, Alex reflected. She hadn't counted on losing her heart again. In some ways she would almost prefer Greg's enmity to this seeming indifference.

'He'll like it,' she stated flatly. 'I've no intention of letting this opportunity slip through my fingers.'

'You aim to stay with *World*?'

'Unless and until something better offers itself.'

He made no comment on that; she hadn't really expected one. Any alternative she might have considered was beyond her reach.

Citrus plantations and terraced fields backed the lovely coastline around Uwajima. The cultured pearl industry was a thriving operation, with large wooden rafts supporting wire cages full of oysters artificially inseminated with the tiny mother-of-pearl bead that in three years' time would form the centre of a perfect hemisphere. Commercially it had to make sense, Alex conceded, but personally she preferred the individuality of the natural pearl.

They found the town itself crowded and festive. After lunch, dubious and reluctant, she accompanied Greg to the stadium where the bullfights were held, relieved to find that, unlike the Spanish version, these were literally tests of strength between animals trained for that sole purpose.

Watching the great, muscular creatures push with interlocked horns until one or the other either turned away or fell to its knees, she was reminded of the *sumo* wrestlers in Kyoto. Not even a week ago yet, she realised. Yuki would be back in Tokyo now. In another couple of days they would no doubt be seeing her again. That had to be Greg's main reason for returning early to the capital—his last opportunity to be with the woman he really loved. Perhaps the hope still lingered that she might at last give in to the emotion they both felt. Whatever the outcome, it would make little difference where she herself was concerned.

'I've had to knock Kochi off the itinerary,' he said when they finally dragged themselves away. 'I want to get well on the road to Kotohira before we stop for the night, so that we can have a fair amount of time at the Shrine tomorrow. You're going to have more than two thousand steps to climb if you want to see the whole thing.'

'I'll manage,' Alex declared. 'That's one place I don't want to miss.' She paused, trying to sound casual about it. 'Whereabouts were you thinking of stopping tonight?'

'Depends how far we get. There's one place we should try, if only for the material it will provide you with.'

'A *ryoken*?'

'Yes, but far more traditional than the one in Tokyo.' His glance was brief. 'We shan't be hitting any towns big enough to have Westernised accommodation on offer, so it's needs must—unless you'd rather sleep in the car?'

Her shrug was meant to signify an indifference of her own. 'Not much point, is there?'

Driving through the town, she watched the passing scene without especial interest. With the Kompira Shrine as a finale she would have more than enough material; the coming few days in Tokyo were going to be superfluous so far as she was concerned. If she could borrow a typewriter she could make a start on the final draft. That would leave Greg free to be with Yuki. There was no actual pain at the thought, just a dull ache in her chest.

The interior of Shikoku was rural to a degree, the dwellings few and far between. Pine forests clothed much of the mountainous landscape. It was getting towards nightfall when they reached the village Greg had been making for.

Smaller than the one in Tokyo, the *ryoken* he had spoken of was situated on a back street. A kimono-clad maid greeted them at the entrance with a polite bow, and

conducted them to a room entered by a sliding door made
of rice paper stretched over a flimsy framework. Screens
of the same material stood in front of the windows, filtering the evening light to an opaque glow. A single
superb painting of a tree occupied the room's mandatory alcove, with freshly cut flowers arranged below.
There were no midway screens to pull, Alex noted in
that first swift perusal. The room wasn't big enough to
be split into two separate halves.

'I know,' she said without particular inflection, when
the maid had left them and before Greg could speak.
'This was all they had.'

'That's right,' he acknowledged. 'We're lucky to get
a room at all, so make the best of it.'

A certain note in his voice drew her eyes to his face,
but there was nothing to be gleaned from his expression.
'I'm afraid there's no private bathroom,' he tagged on.
'You'll have to settle for public ablutions.'

'No problem,' Alex responded, determined to reveal
no further misgivings. 'I don't suppose Japanese women
are all that much different in the skin.'

Blue eyes took on a sudden mocking gleam. 'I don't
suppose Japanese men are either. We're in one of the
few remaining places where mixed bathing is still prac-
tised. Think you can cope?'

Stifling her immediate reactions, she gave him back
look for look. 'Probably better than you'll be able to!'

His laugh was dry. 'You might have a point there.
Anyway, we'd better get moving if we want any dinner.
There's a certain ritual to be observed. Just follow my
lead.'

Short of going without altogether, she had little choice,
Alex conceded. At the very least it would be an experi-

ence worth relating. Greg had seen her nude before, and she him. What difference did it make?

They undressed in an ante-room, depositing their soiled clothing in numbered baskets from where it would be collected, laundered, and returned to them the following morning. Seizing the towel provided and wrapping it loosely about her waist as Greg had done with his, Alex could sense his eyes on her. Standing there, so lean and muscular, he was impossible to ignore.

'So lead on,' she invited in an attempt at insouciance.

'Nobody is going to take any notice,' he said, undeceived by the act. 'Anyone in there is there to bathe, not stare. We each take a stool and a bowl and wash at the taps before getting into the bath itself. The water's going to be hotter than anything you probably ever experienced before, by the way. The secret is to slide in without disturbing it too much, then just close your eyes and relax.'

With him at her side that wasn't going to be easy, she acknowledged wryly. The spirit might be willing but the flesh was having trouble adjusting.

'If it's any consolation,' he said on a suddenly roughened note, 'I'm having the same problem. Let's go and get it over with.'

The size of a small swimming pool, the bath itself already held several people. Close by the entrance door stood a double rank of low units with taps almost at ground level. Men to one side, women to the other, Alex noted in some relief.

Washing all over while seated on one of the tiny stools was difficult, rinsing even more so. As Greg promised, neither of the other two women present took more than a casual interest in her, although they chatted between themselves. Cleansed, they took their towels with them into the bath, wrapping them around their heads once they were in the water to keep their hair out of the way.

Greg was already in. Steeling herself, Alex went to join him, her gasp as she slid down into the steaming liquid involuntary.

'It's boiling!' she exclaimed.

'You'll soon get used to it,' he said. 'Relax.'

She wrapped her hair the way the Japanese had done before doing so, sinking down to a seat on the tiled bottom with her back against the side and closing her eyes. Greg's bare thigh was close enough to feel the hairs brushing her skin. She swallowed thickly, trying to stem the sudden rush of blood to her head. No doubt he wouldn't be averse to making a night of it if she showed the least inclination, but she couldn't afford that kind of indulgence. Getting over him again was going to be difficult enough without making it even harder.

'You're not relaxing,' he said softly. 'I can feel the tension in you from here.'

'It's too hot,' she claimed. 'I can't stand it!'

'You haven't given it a chance. Ten minutes should be enough for a first time, then a cold rinse and you'll feel wonderful.' He nodded to the man just entering the water on his other side. *'Kon-ban-wa.'*

Grinning widely, the newcomer answered with a torrent of rapid-fire Japanese Alex couldn't begin to follow, drawing smiles from those in the immediate vicinity. Greg's response changed those same smiles from amusement at the foreigner's expense to genuine pleasure at the realisation that here was the rarity who not only spoke their language with fluency but could also appreciate their humour. Interest aroused, questions came thick and fast. Alex shrugged a wry apology to a woman who directed one her way, leaving it to Greg to explain her lack of comprehension. Exactly what he did say she had no way of knowing, but it elicited obvious approval.

It was Greg himself in the end who intimated it was time they left the bath. Self-conscious still, Alex rinsed and dried herself swiftly, donning the spotless *yukata* with not a little relief that the ordeal was over. Something different to write about perhaps, but not an experience she could view with the nonchalance Greg seemed able to assume.

Dinner was already waiting for them when they got back to the room, some of the dishes suspended over candle heaters. Reasonably adept by now with the chopsticks, and suddenly ravenous, Alex helped herself liberally to the beef *teriyaki*. Her hair was almost dry, a red-gold cloud about her face. Without make-up she would a short time ago have felt almost naked, but the three days at Usukimiya had given her enough of a tan to disregard such refinements.

Greg was even browner: the strip normally covered by trunks had emphasised the contrast. Remembering brought the familiar curling sensation in the pit of her stomach. One of his legs was stretched beneath the table, his bare foot almost touching hers. Like herself, he was wearing nothing under the *yukata*.

'Feeling good?' he asked unexpectedly, startling her out of her reverie. 'After the bath, I mean.'

'Cleaner than I ever felt,' she acknowledged. 'What was it that woman was asking me?'

His smile was brief. 'She wanted to know if we were on our honeymoon.'

Chest tight, she said, 'So what did you tell her?'

'I said we were taking a second one. She seemed to think it an excellent idea.'

'Why not the truth?' Alex demanded bleakly. 'Scared of what she might think?'

'I doubt if she'd have turned a hair. They've a fairly up-to-date outlook when it comes to non-marital relationships. We should go take a look at one or two of the "love" hotels when we're back in Tokyo. A couple can book a room for just the afternoon. Nice places, too. Nothing cheap.'

'So why lie?' Alex insisted. 'It wouldn't have mattered to me.'

He shrugged. 'Just easier to let it ride, that's all. No harm done.'

Not to him, perhaps, came the thought. If she could only adopt the same attitude of mind!

The maid came in after they finished dinner, first clearing away the used dishes, then returning to lay out the bedding for the night. It was still only a little after ten o'clock, but with a long day ahead of them tomorrow, and conversation at a low ebb, there was nothing to stay up for.

Lying on top of the cover because of the sultry heat, Alex listened to Greg's steady breathing and envied him his ability to switch off at will. Her whole body yearned for his caresses, for his hard muscularity. To be so close and yet so distant was tearing her apart. There had been moments when she had thought he was going to say something—do something—but they'd passed. He was keeping her at arm's length because that was where he wanted her; because he wasn't risking any further involvement; because...

His sudden move to sit up jerked her heart painfully against her ribcage. Motionless, she heard him move across the few feet of *tatami* between them, looking up into shadowed features with breath suspended.

'There's no way we're either of us going to get any sleep until we get *this* out of the way,' he said roughly. 'Don't fight me, Alex, because I'm not in the mood to take rejection. Not when I know it's what you want too.'

'What makes you so sure?' she forced out, and saw the faint grim smile touch his lips.

'That's one sense I haven't lost.'

The *futon* was narrow. Of necessity he had to hold her close. She felt the strength in his arms, closing her eyes as he found her mouth in a kiss that stirred her soul. She was being a fool allowing this to happen again, but she couldn't bring herself to say no. He wasn't going to let her say no anyway.

He opened the *yukata* without lifting his head from hers, sliding his hands the slender, curving length of her body to bring her hips into closer proximity, the hardness in his loins a spur to emotions already threatening to spill over. She moved slowly and sinuously against him, hearing his shortened breath with a sense of glad familiarity. This was how it used to be—how it had always been—the two of them so perfectly attuned to each other's needs.

Leaving her mouth, he moved down her body to take one bare foot and press it to his lips. The light run of his tongue along the sensitive sole drew a moan from deep down in her throat. She twisted frantically to get away from him, but he ignored the resistance, moving on along the side of her foot, her calf, lingering tantalisingly on her inner thigh before lifting to caress the fluttering skin of her belly. He was deliberately holding back, she realised: making her wait his pleasure. There had been a time when he couldn't wait too long himself; when his desire for her had been too intense to control; when the passion had flared between them like a volcano erupting. She wanted to be taken that way now, fast and furiously, driving out the memory of these last two years as if they had never been.

He slid both hands beneath her hips, lifting her to him to convulse her body in sheer sensation. She could hear a voice pleading with him, but it couldn't be hers because she didn't want this to stop, didn't want any of it to stop! Her hands moved over him as he covered her at last, welcoming him into her with urgency, with eagerness, with total abandonment to that mindless ecstasy only Greg could bring...

She came awake again to the strong, pulsing beat of a heart right under her ear, the familiar heaviness of an arm across her back. Sleepily she murmured, 'Did the alarm go off yet?'

'No, the alarm didn't go off.' His voice was low. 'You're dreaming, Alex. Wake up.'

Her eyes came open, examining the firm profile with a swift and dampening recollection. Just a dream, not reality. No amount of wishful thinking could turn back the clock.

'I must have been,' she acknowledged wryly. 'What time is it?'

'Just after six.'

'Is that all?' She attempted a laugh. 'It feels more like midday!' Meeting his eyes, she felt the warmth run under her skin. They had made love again last night before finally falling asleep, the desire mutual and overwhelming. There had to be some emotional involvement left on his side in order to elicit quite that degree of passion.

The words formed themselves. 'Greg, don't let's lose what we've gained.'

The tilt of an eyebrow was his only indication. 'What would you say we have gained?'

Her throat closed up. 'Isn't it obvious?'

'The only thing obvious,' he said with deliberation, 'is that we still share a similar libido. It doesn't make us unique. I'm not going to try making out I fought my inclinations too hard last night. I wanted you badly enough to make that a priority. Only don't let's get carried away either. There's no going back to where we were two years ago.'

'I realise that.' She tried to keep her tone level. 'We're not the same people. All I'm asking is that we stay... friends.'

His laugh had a sardonic edge. 'In bed or out of it?' He put a hand on her arm as she pulled herself abruptly upright away from him, tone suddenly wry. 'Forget I said that.'

Alex was silent, gazing at him, wishing he would haul her down into his arms and kiss her into oblivion again. It seemed to be the only way they could communicate.

His sigh was unexpected. 'We should be moving,' he said. 'We've still some distance to go.'

There was no disputing that point, reflected Alex numbly as he thrust himself upright to reach for his robe. They might have spent the night together, but that was as far as it went. She was wasting her time hoping for any radical change in his attitude towards her. Why not just accept it?

Built on the slopes of Mount Zozusan, the Kompira Shrine was spectacular, with the first flight of over a thousand steps stretching up into the heavens. It was possible to make the upward journey on mule-back, but having watched the somewhat perilous ascent of one couple, Alex opted to walk.

'Don't count them,' warned Greg as they began the climb. 'It only makes things harder.'

It was hard enough anyway, Alex acknowledged ruefully long before they reached the top. Those pilgrims she had read of who did penance for their sins by mounting to the temple on their knees had her full sympathy. It was easy to spot the ones among the crowds of tourists who were doing the pilgrimage around the whole of the island's eighty-eight shrines because they were dressed all in white, although these days they apparently journeyed by bus over a week instead of taking a couple of months to walk round.

The heat was oppressive, the sky taking on a glazed look. She was thankful for the straw hat Greg had purchased for her from a vendor, although he himself went bareheaded as usual. He didn't even appear out of breath, she thought enviously when they finally gained the top.

Looking around the Abbot's lodging, and the Hall of the Morning Sun with its nineteenth century woodcarvings, gave her time to recover both breath and muscle-power before tackling the second flight of around eight hundred steps to the Main Shrine, followed by a further five hundred or so to the Inner Shrine set in a grove of cedar and camphor trees. From here there was a panoramic view of the surrounding countryside, with smaller mountains rising out of the plain like so many pepper pots.

'An hour and a half altogether,' said Greg, consulting his watch. 'It's going to take us two to three hours to make Matsuyama from here, so if we want to get there in daylight we'll need to be on our way by four at the latest.' He paused to snap a group of traditionally-robed *Shinto* priests before they moved out of sight behind a tall wooden fence, bringing his attention back to her as she rested on the stone seat. 'Not as fit as you thought you were?'

'It wouldn't have been as bad if it had been cooler,' she acknowledged wryly. 'I feel like a wet dishrag!'

'You don't look it.' He paused, added on a different note. 'I've been doing some thinking on the way here.'

She winged a swift glance. 'About what?'

'Us,' he said. 'Not that I've reached any far-seeing conclusions. There's no doubt we still have what it takes when it comes to the sexual angle.' His smile was faint. 'I can hardly deny wanting you. The main problem is trust—or lack of it. If we could develop that we might stand a chance of making something worth while in time.'

Alex stared at him, a pulse fluttering at her temple. 'Are you suggesting we get back together again?' she managed at length.

'Isn't that what you were suggesting this morning?'

'I'm...not sure.' She searched the strong features, looking for something she knew she wasn't going to find. 'Isn't this rather a sudden change of heart? Only a few days ago you said there was no chance at all.'

'The question then was, could I feel the same way I used to feel about you? The answer to that is the same.' He was looking out over the view, hands in the pockets of his slacks, expression revealing little. 'You said it yourself: we're two different people. We need to start again from scratch. Maybe we'll make it, maybe we won't. There's only one way to find out.' His shrug was philosophical. 'We don't have anything to lose.'

Except what little peace of mind she had left. came the thought. He hadn't mentioned marriage, of course, yet he had to be thinking along the lines of a possible long-term relationship. That wasn't the stalling point, but what was going to be missing from it. She wanted his love, his whole heart, not just the outer shell.

'What about Yuki?' she asked, unable to hold the question back.

A muscle jerked once at the point of his jaw, the tension immediately relieved. 'Yuki doesn't come into it. How many times do I have to say it? She has her life to lead, I have mine.'

So why the desire to spend three full days in Tokyo if it wasn't to be in her company? came the thought, thrust aside by sheer effort of will. If there was any chance for them at all she had to put Yuki right out of mind. The temptation to throw all caution aside and say yes was great. To be with Greg again on any basis had to be an improvement on not having him at all.

His glance registered the uncertainty in her face, mouth taking on a slant. 'Think about it, anyway. There's no hurry. We'd better start on down before the rain comes, or those steps are going to be treacherous.'

They reached the car just ahead of the rain. Driving through the downpour with the windscreen wipers going full tilt, Greg made no attempt to converse. He had placed the ball fairly and squarely in her court, Alex acknowledged; it was up to her to make the return. How soon he would anticipate an answer she wasn't sure, but an answer there had to be. If only she could convince herself to settle for what was on offer and stop looking for perfection. She might never take Yuki's place in his heart but she could make her own in time to come. She had done it once already, had she only been able to trust it.

The rain stopped after an hour or so, leaving the skies overcast. Without sunlight the landscape looked drab and depressing. By the time they got to Matsuyama it was already dusk. Greg tried three hotels before finally managing to find accommodation.

Walking into the bright and modern foyer in his wake, Alex felt as if she were stepping forwards in time. The realisation that he had secured two separate rooms, albeit next door to each other, left her feeling even more disorientated.

'I thought we both needed the breathing space,' he said levelly outside her door. 'I'll see you downstairs for dinner in an hour.'

Alone in the well-appointed room, Alex took out the one uncrushable dress from her suitcase and hung it ready to slip into after her shower. The bathroom seemed so tiny by comparison with the one she had used the previous night—and lonely. Her face in the mirror looked different, she thought: as if the happenings of the past two weeks had stamped an indelible mark. For the first time in days she applied full make-up, brushing her hair into gleaming smoothness.

The fine pleating of the pale beige dress outlined a figure that seemed a little more slender than usual. Not so surprising considering how little she had been eating overall, she supposed. She tightened her belt another hole before sliding her feet into the high-heeled sandals, gave herself another critical glance in the mirror, and knew she could delay the moment no longer.

Clad in the same off-white suit and dark blue shirt he had worn that evening in Tokyo, Greg was waiting for her in the lobby. He was studying the window display of one of the in-house shops when she stepped from the lift, and drawing the unconcealed interest of a European woman seated on her own in a nearby alcove. He quirked an eyebrow fleetingly in the latter's direction as he turned on Alex's approach, the faint smile still playing about his lips.

'Back to normal again?'

'More or less,' she said. 'Are we eating here?'

He shook his head. 'I thought we might have a change. Do you like Italian food?'

'Well, yes.' She added quickly, 'Only don't feel obliged for my sake.'

'For mine, then,' he said. 'I fancy a lasagne.' He ran a discerning eye over her. 'You've some weight to make up before we go home.'

It wasn't the only thing she had to make up, reflected Alex as she moved with him towards the hotel entrance. She was no nearer any hard and fast decision on that score.

They went by taxi to the restaurant in the city centre, having had the car picked up by the hire company earlier. The place was packed with both European and Japanese clientele. Greg, however, had telephoned from the hotel to reserve a table in advance.

'Forward planning in everything,' Alex commented on a light note when they were seated with drinks in front of them and menus to hand.

'Not everything,' he denied. 'Plans don't always work out. The *spiedino* sounds good for starters, don't you think?'

'I'm not all that hungry,' she said truthfully. 'I'll just have the lasagne.' She cast a comprehensive glance around, taking in the wholly authentic ambience of the place. 'You'd hardly believe we were still in Japan!'

'This time on Monday we'll be on our way home,' he rejoined. 'I'll expect an answer before then.'

Alex looked across at him a little helplessly, wishing she could read the mind behind that vivid gaze. 'Are you sure it's what you want?'

His smile was fleeting. 'I'd hardly be suggesting it otherwise. I'll be thirty-five next month. Time I took stock of my life and where I'm going. There hasn't been anyone to speak of since you walked out.'

'Don't keep reminding me.' She hesitated before adding slowly, 'Were you really planning on asking me to marry you, Greg?'

The dark head inclined. 'Eventually.'

Her breath came out on a long sigh. 'Until I ruined everything.'

'So we give ourselves a second chance.' He said it without expression. 'We already proved we're compatible in at least one department.'

'You won't be expecting me to...move in with you?'

'Not immediately. I jumped the gun once, I shan't make that mistake again.' He lifted a questioning brow. 'Do I take it you're saying yes?'

She hadn't intended saying anything. Not yet. Only it was too late now to start backing out. 'I suppose I am,' she said slowly, and drew a dry smile.

'It's a free choice. If you're not prepared to put any effort into it...'

'I am!' On impulse, she reached across to lay her hand over his, senses stirring to the mere feel of him. 'I really am, Greg.'

He turned his hand over so that hers lay in his palm, his clasp firm. There was no mockery in his smile, just a certain rueful quality. 'Time will tell.'

The lasagne was excellent, the wine full and fruity. Alex took care not to overindulge in either. Greg couldn't really intend they should spend the night apart, she reasoned. Not now they had things sorted out between them. She couldn't wait to have his arms about her, his mouth on hers, driving out doubt the way only he could. Not a lasting remedy perhaps, but a reassurance of sorts. Where physical contact was concerned, they were in perfect harmony.

They danced a couple of times to the music of the small resident group. Closing her eyes, Alex could almost imagine the past two years had never happened. In a little while they would be going home to bed, making love with that delicious abandonment they had known from the very first time. She could make him love her again if she set her mind to it; she was suddenly filled with the certainty of it. This time they were going to stay together.

It was almost midnight when they returned to the hotel. Going up in the lift, walking along the corridor, Alex waited for Greg to intimate which room they would be sharing for the rest of the night. When he paused outside her own door and held out a hand for the key, she had it ready and waiting, her heart beating a rapid tattoo on the wall of her chest.

'There you are,' he said, pushing open the door and handing the key back to her. 'I've ordered a taxi to the airport for eight-thirty, so it's breakfast no later than seven forty-five.' He studied her face for a moment as if waiting for her comment, shoulders lifting briefly when she failed to say anything. 'Sleep well.'

Alone again inside the room, Alex leaned on the door and wondered where she had gone wrong. Had the whole thing been a cruel joke on his part—a deliberate humiliation?

Not possible, she tried to comfort herself. No one could change their whole character. But then, why?

She was undressed and ready to slide into the empty bed when the possible reason hit her. So far Greg had been the one to instigate lovemaking between them. Perhaps what he was looking for was some initiative on her part—some sign of that effort she had promised to make.

The only way to find out was to put theory to test. Mentally squaring her shoulders, she went over and knocked softly on the communicating door. If she was wrong, the humiliation would be complete, but she would weather it. Anything was better than lying awake all night wondering.

He was minus his shirt but nothing else when he opened the door. The blue eyes regarded her steadily.

'I was just beginning to think the message had failed to get through,' he said.

Alex tilted her chin a fraction, still not wholly certain of his mood. 'Is this your way of bringing me to heel?'

Amusement lit his gaze. 'If that's what you want to call it. I don't intend making all the running.' He paused, brow lifting. 'Are you coming through here, or do I come through there?'

'Here,' she said, feeling suddenly and ridiculously shy of him.

It didn't last, of course. He saw to that. But it felt strange, and not particularly comfortable, to be in a proper bed again. Alex found herself missing the firmness beneath her spine. Wakening in Greg's arms in the grey light that preceeded the dawn, she knew a sudden depression at the thought of returning to Tokyo. Being in Yuki's company wasn't going to help any of them.

There was going to be a whole lot of speculation aroused among friends and colleagues back home when word got around. Greg was already known to several of the former as her one-time partner. Had she been as confident of his love as she was now of hers for him, then none of it would matter. Playing second fiddle wasn't going to come easy.

He murmured something unintelligible in his sleep, the arm lying across her waist moving to draw her closer. She could feel his breath on her cheek, the rasp of morning stubble along his jawline, the excruciating tickle of his chest hair against her breasts.

Without thinking about it, she put her lips to the strong brown column of his throat, pressing them softly into the hollow at its base. He stirred again, coming awake to look into her eyes with the fire already stoked in his. When he rolled he took her with him, hands sliding about her with a possessiveness that thrilled her, holding her to him while he kissed her with the passion so long remembered. While they still had this she could cope with the rest, she thought, then gave herself up to the emotions running riot within her.

CHAPTER EIGHT

UNLIKE Narita, Tokyo's domestic airport, Haneda, was only fifteen minutes from the city centre. Alex was pleased to discover they were booked into the same *ryoken* again.

'I was hoping for this,' she confessed when the maid had departed. 'Last night just wasn't the same!'

Greg lifted an expressive eyebrow. 'Where did I fail?'

This was the old Greg, she thought: bantering, easy. She answered in the same vein. 'As if you could!'

'There's a first time for everything,' he said. 'I'm not as young as I used to be.'

'Oh, one foot in the grave already!' Meeting his glance she felt emotion flood her, swift and sweet. 'What's on the agenda for this afternoon?' she asked hastily before impulse could take over.

'Lunch first, then shopping. We didn't get to do Mitsokoshi last time. That's an experience in itself. There must be things you'd like to buy while you're here?'

'One or two,' Alex admitted. She turned away to find her toilet bag, adding over a shoulder, 'How about later?'

'We're going out for the evening with Yuki and Shige,' he returned. 'Tokyo by night. You can't leave that out of your reckoning.'

'I don't suppose so.' She slid the zip of her suitcase closed again. 'When did you arrange that?'

'This morning, while you were in the shower.'

'You telephoned her?'

'I couldn't get hold of a carrier pigeon.'

Alex bit her lip, aware of meriting the irony. 'All right, stupid thing to say. Did you . . . tell her?'

He made no pretence of not understanding her meaning. 'I told her.'

'How did she react?'

The sigh was audible 'She wished the two of us luck— or words to that effect What would you expect her to have said?'

It was a rhetorical question: at least. Alex treated it as such. It was pretty obvious. she thought hollowly, that his emotions were still very much involved with the other woman. She was going to have to be strong-minded herself to put that knowledge aside.

They ate a lunch of crisp, deep-fried delicacies at Ten-Ichi-Honten in the Ginza. The party at the adjoining table were foreigners, loud-mouthed and arrogant in their criticism of everything brought to them.

'People like that shouldn't be allowed to travel overseas!' declared Alex with feeling, thoroughly incensed by the performance. 'How on earth does that waiter keep his cool?'

'The smile on the face of the tiger,' Greg said drily. 'He's probably contemplating poisoning the lot of them underneath. You get that type in every nationality, unfortunately. I've come across one or two English who shouldn't be let loose either.'

He summoned the waiter to fetch the bill, bringing a genuine smile to the man's face with a few obviously sympathetic words when he did so. They were bowed to the door of the restaurant like royalty, and urged to return.

'You're accepted here, aren't you?' Alex observed as they threaded a passage along the crowded pavement. 'Speaking the language opens all doors.'

'Some,' he corrected. 'I told you before, it doesn't work like that. I'm not Japanese. No matter how close the friendship, that's still the ruling factor.'

And the reason why Yuki wouldn't marry him, she thought. For her own sake, she supposed she should be grateful.

One of Tokyo's largest department stores, Mitsukoshi was situated right at the heart of the Ginza. The imposing entrance hall had a vast sculpture rising from the centre of the grand central staircase.

'The Goddess of Sincerity,' said Greg. 'Here to reassure the customer that they're getting a square deal. If you're thinking of taking back a *yukata* they'll be on either the third or fourth floor.'

A smartly dressed and smiling young man came over to greet them, leading the way to the lifts and summoning the cage for them before bowing out again. They weren't the only ones receiving VIP treatment. The American couple who arrived just as the doors were closing were voluble in their praise of Japanese courtesy. They sure didn't have anything like it back home in New York, the woman declared.

There was a whole department devoted to kimonos, from the plain and functional to the gloriously festive. The prices of the latter were exorbitant, the garment itself totally impractical for leisure-wear. Alex settled in the end on a fine cotton in the traditional blue and white.

'I'm surprised you don't have one already,' she said casually to Greg as they waited for the purchase to be wrapped.

'I don't keep Japanese memorabilia around back home,' came the equally casual reply. 'Everything in its place. There's an art exhibition on eight, if you're interested—even a *Shinto* temple on the roof. We'll need to leave time to get back and change before we meet Yuki and Shige, so anything else you want you'd better get now.'

Alex had forgotten about the coming evening over the last hour or two. The reminder brought sudden deflation. It was bad enough knowing the way the two of them felt about each other; to spend several hours in company with it was going to tax her emotions to the limit. For a brief moment she toyed with the idea of backing out, but had to acknowledge that finding a plausible excuse was next to impossible. Greg had arranged this for her benefit—or so he made out. She would just have to put a brave face on it.

They were back at the *ryoken* before five. Greg had sent his suit to be valeted that morning. Pristine fresh, it was waiting in their room, along with the green silk dress Alex had had pressed.

'I'm going to miss this kind of service,' she confessed, sorting out clean underwear. 'It's back to the launderette next week.'

'Providing Ben doesn't have another job lined up for you.' The tone was easy, but with an underlying note that drew her eyes. 'I've a feeling you're going to be doing a lot of travelling from now on.'

She said slowly, 'You're not suggesting I should change my job, by any chance?'

'I'm not suggesting anything,' he returned. 'Now might be a good time to mention, though, that if we do make a go of it, it has to be on a permanent footing this time.'

Alex looked at him with a steadiness she was far from feeling. 'You mean . . . marriage?'

'I mean marriage.' He paused, his voice taking on an added emphasis. 'I'd want a real one, Alex. Along with all the things that go with it.'

'Such as?' Her own voice sounded amazingly calm.

'Children, for one.' Humour briefly widened his mouth. 'Or preferably a couple. I was an only child myself. I don't recommend it.'

'You're going too fast,' she protested. 'I hadn't even thought that far ahead!'

'But you have to know *how* you feel about it.'

'Well, yes, I suppose so.' The words came hesitantly. 'I'd like children, of course, only...'

'Only?' he prompted as her voice trailed away.

Alex pulled herself sharply together. They were discussing possible eventualities, not certainties. She could make an honest answer. 'I'd need to be sure we were going to stay together. It's the children who suffer most in a divorce.'

'If we marry,' he said with deliberation, 'we'll stay together.'

The operative word being 'if', she reflected. He hadn't mentioned love, but then, why should he? Yuki held the monopoly on that emotion.

She said huskily, 'You can't build a marriage on physical attraction, Greg.'

'Others have done it on less.' He studied her averted face for a moment before sliding a hand around the back of her neck beneath the fall of hair. His kiss stirred her as always, rousing her to respond despite herself. When he lifted his head again she felt bereft. 'We can make it,' he said.

Only because he was willing to settle for half the loaf, she thought. Whether it would be enough for her too was something she was going to have to think about long and hard before making any final commitment.

The 'restaurant' where they were to eat dinner proved to be a small, dark place hidden down a narrow back alley. Yuki and Shige already awaited their arrival in a private room furnished in traditional style and floored in *tatami*.

Looking beautiful in figured silk, Yuki greeted both of them with equal pleasure, kissing Greg on the lips and Alex on the cheek. Less accustomed to Western informality, Shige contented himself with the usual polite bow.

'It seems so long since we were last together,' Yuki exclaimed when they were all seated around the low table nibbling from dishes of tempting appetisers as a preliminary to the main meal. 'You must tell us all you did and saw this last week.'

Alex was content to let Greg do most of the telling, occasionally stirring herself to put in a comment. Shige was interested in everything—or pretended to be. Like the waiter at lunch time, his smile masked all inner reaction.

A good-looking man, she acknowledged, and obviously an intelligent one. Just a friend, Yuki had called him. She wondered if that was all he felt for her. Certainly they were very good friends. That much at least was apparent from the way they spoke to each other, the way they were at ease with one another. Perhaps, she mused, in time to come the two of them might develop a deeper feeling. Yuki might be strong enough to deny herself the man she loved because of a simple accident of birth, but that didn't mean she intended spending the rest of her life alone, any more than Greg did.

All else aside, she had to admire the way they both handled the situation. No one who didn't know would ever suspect the hidden emotion. Only to her was there an occasional fleeting sadness in the almond eyes. Greg had shot his last bolt by announcing their own renewed relationship. If that hadn't softened Yuki's attitude nothing ever would, and he knew it. Hence the decision to sound her out on the domestic scene. He needed someone to share his life—to provide him with all the things most other men of his age already had by now. It was largely up to her from here on in, she realised. If she wanted him he was hers, in body if not wholly in spirit.

It was almost ten o'clock when they left the *ryoriya*. Buzzing with life and laden with the smell of hot *sake* and barbecued chicken, the street outside had become another world. There was even a fortune-teller seated at a little table with lantern and charts. Someone was playing the *shamisen* somewhere close by, the staccato notes suddenly drowned by disco music as a door opened to emit a gang of laughing youths.

Round a corner, and they were straight into the neon-lit extravaganza that was the Ginza by night. Greg hadn't bothered to bring a camera. He already had dozens of shots of the night-time scene from previous visits.

'I'd rather like to visit a nightclub,' Alex requested as the four of them moved along the thronged and noisy thoroughfare. 'Just for local colour. No one has to get up too early in the morning, do they?'

It was Yuki who answered, tone apologetic. 'The nightclubs are for men.'

Alex looked at her in genuine astonishment. 'You mean women are actually banned?'

'It's a tacit understanding,' Greg put in. 'It always has been. You'd be allowed in but you wouldn't be comfortable.' His mouth firmed as she started to protest. 'We don't go. That's it.'

'We could visit a disco if you like,' offered Yuki, obviously anxious to make amends. 'There are many from which to choose. Or perhaps we might return to my apartment for coffee?' Her smile was for Greg. 'You see, I have acquired many Western habits!'

'Only the best ones,' he returned. 'And it sounds an excellent way to round off the evening.' He had a hand up almost before he finished speaking, hailing a cruising taxi.

Alex was silent during the ride, furious with Greg's high-handed treatment. So how had she been expected to know that women didn't frequent nightclubs in this part of the world? Not second-class citizens, he had stated that afternoon back in the office. What did he call this kind of discrimination?

She made sure not to offer help in the preparation of the coffee when they reached the apartment in case that was a no-go area too. Still not fully at ease with them, Shige made polite conversation about the city and its environs. Greg's admittance that he had never done the Fuji-san pilgrimage elicited surprise. In one more week the season would be over, the paths to the summit closed until the following July. For her needs, Alex gathered, the experience was not to be missed.

Yuki expressed some doubt when the question was put to her. The way to the top was hard and long, she said. They would need to set out in the afternoon and spend the night in one of the stone shelters built for the purpose if they wished to see the sunrise.

'But worth it,' Alex insisted, unwilling to allow the opportunity to pass. 'Our flight isn't until late Monday evening. We'll be back in Tokyo by early afternoon at the latest.'

'And tired,' Greg pointed out.

'So what?' Her tone was still a little short with him. 'We can sleep on the plane.' She added coolly, 'I'd have thought it too good a chance to miss, considering what we're primarily here for.'

'Why should we not all four make the expedition?' asked Shige into the pause. 'It has been many years since I was there.'

'I do not think...' began Yuki.

'Oh, you *have* to come,' Alex interrupted smoothly. 'It wouldn't be the same without you!'

If the other registered the sarcasm she wasn't revealing it. Her smile and bow were in no way exaggerated. 'Thank you, Alex.'

An angry glint in his eyes, Greg said with emphasis, 'Then that's settled. We'll need to leave fairly early, I imagine. It must be at least a couple of hours by train to the base.'

'We will travel in my brother's car,' declared Shige, more voluble than he had been all evening. 'That way we can drive to the fifth station, and take only five hours to make the climb instead of nine.'

Five hours! thought Alex, beginning to have some doubts of her own regarding this venture. There was coming down again too. Catching Yuki's eye, she tried to convey apology for her tartness a few moments ago. The other's heartache might be concealed, but that didn't mean it was any less painful. Her own fault or not, she was losing the man she loved to another woman.

'We shall need warm clothing,' Shige was saying now. 'It will be cold at the summit. And food too. It is far too expensive to buy on the way.' He added modestly, 'All this I can arrange.'

'So all we need now is a good night's sleep to set us up for the hard work to come,' said Greg. 'Which seems to indicate an end to the evening. Mind if I phone for a taxi, Yuki?'

Her smile held a sudden hint of mischief. 'Be my guest, Wilde *san*.'

Shige accompanied them down to the street. He lived not too far away and liked to walk, he said, when Greg offered to drop him off. He would be at the *ryoken* at eleven to pick them up.

There was no conversation in the taxi. Greg seemed remote again, profile austere against the passing lights. They were in their room before he finally spoke his mind.

'You could learn a lot from the Japanese. Politeness costs nothing.'

'I wasn't aware I'd been anything else but,' Alex replied stubbornly. 'So I made a gaffe over the nightclub business...'

'I'm not talking about that,' he cut in. 'Although if you'd done your homework you'd have known it wasn't on. Yuki deserves better than you dished out to her tonight.'

Alex felt her throat go tight. 'I suppose you could put it down to jealousy,' she said on a cool note.

'There's nothing to be jealous of.' He sounded clipped, curt. 'She and I never slept together, if that's what's bothering you.'

No, she thought painfully, their love was on a higher plane! She made an effort to regain lost ground. 'So I'll apologise in the morning for anything I said that may have upset her.'

There was a pause. When he spoke again it was with a certain weariness. 'Just let it go. She'd be mortified to think she'd given her feelings away.'

'It isn't going to work, is it?' she said thickly as he began to take off his clothing. 'It just isn't going to work!'

He stopped what he was doing to look across at her, expression controlled. 'Does that mean you want out again?'

'Do you?' she asked.

'No.' The flat statement left no margin for doubt. He moved to take hold of her by the shoulders, forcing her to look him in the eye. 'We need each other, Alex. That's a good enough basis to start from.'

His kiss was far from gentle, but it wasn't gentleness she wanted from him. She kissed him back with a kind of desperation, sliding her arms up and around his neck to hold him close. If passion was all he felt at present then she would settle for that. She would settle for anything rather than lose him again. Yuki had never known this side of him—never would know this side of him. It was an advantage of a kind.

Shige collected Yuki first before coming on the *ryoken*. He had brought warm sweaters for both of them, together with waterproof capes such as cyclists might wear in case the weather took a turn for the worse. These would also serve as windcheaters when the sun went down and the temperature dropped.

The more Alex heard about the forthcoming trip, the less enthusiastic she felt, but it was too late now to start raising objections. Seated in the rear of the car with Yuki, she took extra care to be friendly during the journey.

After last night, she told herself, hugging the memory to her, she could afford to be generous. Greg's love-making had been so totally and utterly wonderful. This time it was going to work out; she was sure of it. Yuki might always hold a place in his heart, but she was going to be his wife—the mother of his children in time to come. He would learn to love her again, the way she loved him.

Mostly hidden by smog from Tokyo itself, Mount Fuji in close-up was a splendid, awe-inspiring sight. Even in these hottest days of the Japanese summer, snow still lingered in places at the summit.

They made the fifth station, about half-way up the mountain, by one-thirty. From here there was a superb view of the five Fuji lakes around the northern base. Alex was astonished to see the numbers and variety of people setting out to make the climb. In age they ranged from children scarcely more than toddlers to those who had to be in their seventies at least. There was even a small group of blind men roped together and led by two sighted guides.

At first the route upwards didn't seem too steep. At the sixth station they were joined by more people climbing via the Yoshida route. Pilgrimage it might be, quiet and contemplative it wasn't. Voices filled the clear air.

Greg paused often to take photographs, not only of the ever unfolding views but of the people around them.

'You should publish what Ben doesn't use yourself,' suggested Alex casually at one point. 'An inside view of Japan from an outsider with special privileges.'

'That is a good idea, Greg,' agreed Yuki, overhearing. 'Perhaps Alex herself could be persuaded to write the text for you.'

'I didn't mean that,' disclaimed Alex hastily. 'He could write his own text.'

'Without your flair for it,' he returned. 'It's something we can talk about when we get back. Ben won't be using more than eight or nine shots at the most.'

Alex stole a glance at Yuki. The other's face was quite serene, but that wasn't to say she felt nothing. She was quite deliberately pushing her and Greg together, regardless of how much it might hurt. Greg must realise it too, although he showed no reaction. His years in Japan must have given him the ability to conceal his emotions so well, Alex reflected wryly. There was just no way of telling what his thoughts really were.

The way became steeper, harder, the temperature falling with each hundred feet gained in height. At one point it was necessary to haul oneself along by chains sunk into the rock. At each station there were shops selling souvenirs and refreshments, but with full darkness due to fall around seven-thirty, there was little time to stop and rest.

Of the four of them, Alex was bound to acknowledge, she was the least able to take the strain. Her legs felt like jelly already, her chest tight as a drum, and she was beginning to feel the cold seeping through her clothing. Not even the view could fully compensate for what she was going through, although not for anything did she intend admitting it. What Yuki Nagasowa could do, she could do—if she died in the attempt. At the moment, she thought with rueful humour, that didn't seem all that remote a possibility!

There was accommodation in stone huts available at both seventh and eighth stations. Greg chose to continue to the latter on the basis of having less ground to cover in the morning. The huts themselves were communal, and quite basic, with space allocated on *tatami* mats for a fee. Most people had brought their own food and drink, and set to quite happily to make the most of it.

Seated with her back against the wall and fingers stretched to the Calor gas stove Shige had had the forethought to bring, Alex tried to forget how cold and tired she was and join in the general conversation. Yuki seemed as fresh as when they had set out, her face animated as she talked. Occasionally the three of them lapsed into Japanese for a sentence or two, leaving Alex feeling totally isolated. It was just, Greg explained, that some things simply couldn't be said in English.

Gradually people began drifting off to sleep. Dozing herself, Alex came awake with a start when Greg slid an arm around her and drew her close.

'Warmer this way,' he said.

On the other side, Yuki was lying down with face turned away, Shige beyond her. Alex felt real sympathy for her predicament. No matter how generous the spirit, it couldn't be easy to see the man one loved with his arm around another woman.

'Finding it rough?' he murmured as she relaxed against him with a sigh.

'I'll cope,' she said, and forced a lighter note. 'At least going down has to be easier!'

'And quicker.' For a brief moment his lips were pressed to her temple, finding the rapidly beating pulse. 'Try and sleep. We'll be on our way again before three if we want to see the sunrise from the summit.'

She did sleep eventually, wakening to find Greg's arm gone, although he was still comfortably close. He was talking to Yuki, she realised, the two of them keeping their voices low, the murmur only just reached her ears. Even if they had been speaking in English she wouldn't have been able to distinguish the actual words, she thought, but it took little imagination to guess what they were saying. In a few hours they would be parting again, this time perhaps for ever. Could she begrudge either of them the chance to say what was in their hearts?

Yes, if she were honest, she could, came the answer, only it wasn't in her to break in on the moment either. Her time would come when they were home again in England. Until then, she would try to be as forbearing as Yuki herself was being over the whole affair.

Rising while it was still dark outside took every ounce of will-power she possessed. It was bitterly cold in the open, the wind fierce. The cape afforded some protection from the latter around her upper half but, despite slacks and stout walking shoes, her legs and feet felt frozen.

'You'll be OK once we get going,' said Greg with what she considered scant sympathy, seeing her shiver. 'You wanted to come.'

'You don't need remind me,' she groaned. 'I must have been mad!'

'It will be worth it when you see the sunrise,' Shige assured her. 'There is no sight more beautiful in the whole of Japan!'

It would have to be magnificent indeed to compensate for this, Alex reflected, but kept her mouth shut.

They reached the summit just before the half-hour to find the area already swarming with people. Some of them, Yuki said, would have climbed through the night in order to save themselves the price of accommodation.

The sky to the west was tinged with pink, the colour slowly growing and spreading until the first golden ray topped the horizon to a concerted shout of *Banzai!* from the assembly. Far below, the emerging landscape stretched to the far distant Pacific, a stunning vista of countryside, peninsulas, islands.

Greg wasn't the only photographer around, but certainly the only foreign one that Alex could see. He was totally engrossed. Taking out her notebook, she attempted to get down her impressions, although no matter which way she described the scene it was going to sound trite, she acknowledged.

Shige looked gratified when she expressed her appreciation. 'You are glad now that you came?' he asked.

'Very,' Alex assured him, and then with a smile, 'Not that I might not change my mind again when it comes to going down!'

'We'll have to leave around eight if we want to get back to Tokyo in time to change and have a meal before making for the airport,' said Greg, finishing off a film. 'That gives us roughly three hours up here. I want to take a look at the crater for starters.'

Alex stirred herself as he glanced her way. Tired or no, she wasn't about to miss out on anything. 'Lead on,' she invited. 'I can't do worse than fall in.'

His sudden grin was heartwarming. 'I'll keep an eye on you.'

An arm would be better, she thought, longing for his touch. The sooner they got down from this mountain, the sooner they could be on their own again. Not even the thought of that long flight could deter her, because they would be on their way to a whole new life together. It was going to be a good one too; she was determined on that. No backsliding where Yuki was concerned. That was over and done with.

Quiescent for more than two hundred and fifty years, the volcano bowl was just a stony valley laced with scrubby patches of grass. Interesting to the geologist, perhaps, Alex conceded, but rather disappointing to her mind. In the end she found a sheltered spot and sat down to wait until the others were ready to start the return journey, too cold to make any further effort.

Shige came to join her some ten minutes later. Without bothering to ask, he brought out the little stove and set water to boil. Minus both milk and sugar though it was, to Alex, nectar itself couldn't have tasted better than the steaming hot coffee he eventually produced.

'You're a godsend!' she exclaimed gratefully, feeling the warmth curling through her. 'Yuki is fortunate to have you as a friend, Shige.' She hadn't consciously planned the question, but the words were out before she fully realised the intention. 'Or is there more than just friendship between you?'

There was no anger or resentment in his expression. When he answered his voice was calm and level, the statement matter-of-fact. 'There can never be anything but friendship between us.'

'Because she loves ... someone else?'

Shige inclined his head. 'It is a sad affair.'

It was a pointless exercise, but something in her couldn't let the subject go. She said softly, 'Surely the remedy is in her own hands?'

'Only if she is prepared to sacrifice the regard of her family, and it is doubtful she would ever do that.' His shrug was dismissive. 'It is not a matter you would readily understand. Would you like some more coffee?'

Alex shook her head. For the first time she felt a pang of real sympathy for the woman who felt honour-bound to sacrifice her personal happiness to the edicts of her culture. If she had anything to do with it, Greg would one day get over her, but would Yuki ever get over Greg?

The two of them were coming back, neither revealing the dejection they must be experiencing at the thought of the coming parting.

'I've got everything I need,' Greg declared, accepting a mug of coffee, 'so we can make tracks as soon as we've finished this.' Blue eyes sought green, the expression in them hard to define. 'Just fourteen hours and we'll be on our way home. Think you can bear up that long?'

'I can but try,' she rejoined with forced brightness.

Going down the mountain proved scarcely less arduous than coming up, although it got steadily warmer as they descended. By the time they reached the sixth station they were able to take off their sweaters and feel the sun warming their skin. Looking back at the summit now wreathed in cloud, Alex could scarcely believe they had actually stood up there on the top of the world.

'It gives a real sense of achievement,' she admitted when they were in the car at last and heading back towards Tokyo. 'Ben will never believe I actually climbed the thing!'

'He'll have expected it of you,' commented Greg drily. 'I'd say he expects all things of all people. I wonder what he'll have in store for you next?'

'Nothing too strenuous, I hope,' she responded. Nor too far away, she added mentally. Not yet, at any rate.

They stopped off for a meal on the way, arriving in Tokyo towards four o'clock in the afternoon. Greg had booked the extra day on their room in order to give them a place to bathe and change their clothing before making for the airport. After dropping them off, Yuki and Shige continued on to change their own clothing, the latter promising to pick them up again at six-thirty.

'They're both coming to see us off?' asked Alex as they made their way to the room for the last time.

'Considering they didn't say goodbye yet, that seems likely,' Greg responded. 'Any reason why not?'

'Just that it's a long way out there, and back again, and I thought they'd be too tired, that's all, she disclaimed. 'I'm just about shattered myself!'

'*Too* shattered?' he asked softly, sliding the door at his back.

Heart jerking, she turned to meet his gaze, limbs turning to water at the look in his eyes. A part of her wanted to go to him, to feel his arms come around her, so strong and comforting, but she couldn't bring herself to make the move. No matter how much she tried to tell herself it didn't matter, Yuki was still there between them. Only when the two of them finally said *sayonara* might she be able to put it aside.

'I still have to finish packing,' she said. 'Supposing you take your bath while I do it?'

His lips twisted. 'Sounds good practical sense.'

Left alone, Alex laid out the tan linen suit and accessories she was to travel in, and did a totally unnecessary reorganisation of her suitcase. She had known all along that her hold on Greg was physically orientated, she thought depressedly, so why start carping about it now? It was up to her to deepen that emotion into something more meaningful, and that was going to take time. Rejecting him wasn't going to help.

All the same, she made no attempt to go to him. When he emerged from the bathroom, shaved and ready all but his outer clothing, he seemed in total command of himself. Only when she briefly met his glance in passing did she register the lack of warmth.

'It's all yours,' he said. 'You have over an hour.'

They were waiting in the entrance hall when the car arrived. The proprietor himself saw them off the premises, bowing so low his forehead almost touched the ground. This time Yuki was sitting up front at Shige's side, leaving Alex and Greg to share the rear of the car. Not that she need have bothered, Alex wryly conceded. The relationship had taken a distinct turn for the worse.

With the evening traffic heavy and congested, it took them over two hours to drive the sixty-five kilometres out to Narita. Once checked in at the desk, and freed of all but carry-on luggage, there was time to retire to a bar for a final and farewell drink before going through to the departure lounge.

Never the chatterbox, Yuki was even quieter than usual. With Greg making little contribution to conversation either, Alex felt it incumbent on her to keep things going. Her brightness was overdone, and she knew it, but it was that or nothing.

It was a relief when their flight was called. Goodbyes were brief and unemotional on all sides. Face expressionless, Greg didn't look back as they walked away from the Japanese couple.

Only when they were through passport control, and heading for the gate did Alex begin to unwind a little. It was just the two of them now. She could cope with that—she hoped.

CHAPTER NINE

IT WAS raining when they landed. Greg left Alex with the luggage while he went to fetch the car round.

'Miserable morning,' he commented when they were on their way at last. 'Cold, too, compared with where we just came from.' He glanced her way briefly. 'Still tired?'

She had slept for much of the sixteen-hour flight, but it hadn't really rested her, Alex conceded. 'Pretty much,' she acknowledged. 'I suppose it's going to take a day or two to catch up.'

'More like the rest of the week, from past experience. Is Ben going to be prepared to wait that long for your stuff?'

She laughed. 'No way! I'm due at the office Thursday morning at the latest with a final draft.'

'Think you can do it?'

'With a little application. The shape is there already.' She added lightly, 'It might be a good idea if you went over it for me before I submit, just to make sure I didn't get anything wrong.'

'I shouldn't think there's much danger,' he returned.

Her eyes were drawn fleetingly to the lean features etched in relief against the tunnel lights, her heart contracting. They were like a couple of strangers again, and she wasn't sure what to do about it. Yuki hadn't been left behind; she was right here in the car with them.

'You'll have to point me in the right direction for your place,' he said without taking his eyes from the windscreen. 'What is it, a flat?'

'Yes. Ground floor. I moved out there when I got this job with *World*. I couldn't have afforded it before.'

'It isn't shared, then?'

'No.' She laughed. 'It isn't very big, either. Just one room with convertible, kitchenette and bath.'

'What else do you need?'

It was making conversation for the sake of it, but she had to keep on or let depression swamp her. 'Not a lot, I suppose. It's a hundred per cent better than the last couple of places. I was lucky to get it—especially at such a fair rent. The man who owns the house seems more interested in the kind of people he leases to than the money itself.'

'A rarity indeed.'

Alex went on talking about nothing in particular for the rest of the journey. At this hour the traffic was minimal. Greg carried her bag into the hallway of the big old house in Wimbledon, but declined her invitation to stay for coffee.

'We both need some decent sleep,' he said. His kiss was almost perfunctory. 'I'll phone you later.'

She waited until she heard the car pull away before putting her key in her door lock, feeling the threatened depression overtaking her. Partially jet-lag, of course. The sooner someone came up with a real antidote for this mental dislocation the better! Greg hadn't seemed to suffer at all, in either direction—but then who could tell just what did go on in that dark head?

The best accommodation she had known since first coming to work in London it might be, but in the dull morning light the whole place looked dull and dreary:

overcrowded with furniture. She found herself missing
the clean and simple lines of the Japanese living-room,
the feel of *tatami* under her feet. She was missing Greg
too—and uncertain of his attitude. Perhaps he already
regretted his offer to start over again.

Bed, she told herself wearily at that point. Things
might look better after a good long rest.

She was asleep almost before her head touched the
pillow, awakening what seemed like bare moments later
to the burr of the telephone on the bedside table. Greg
sounded faint and far away.

'Just surfaced?'

'Yes,' Alex admitted, still not fully in possession of
her faculties. 'What time is it?'

'Six o'clock,' he said, bringing memory into sudden
sharp focus. He added, 'Look, I'm going to be pretty
tied up getting things straight round here this next day
or so. Supposing we meet for lunch on Thursday? That
will give both of us chance to sort ourselves out.'

From somewhere Alex summoned the necessary
smoothness of tone. 'Sounds a good idea. What time?'

'Twelve-thirty—L'Escargot?'

'Fine.' She gave a mock yawn. 'Sorry, I'm still not
firing on all cylinders! Bye, Greg.'

Replacing the receiver, she sat with head bowed on to
bent knees for a moment or two, fighting the wave of
despair. There was no point in looking on the black side
of things. Not until Greg made it plain that he had
changed his mind about their future together. He
couldn't have, she comforted herself. Not this fast. He
might be having doubts, but they could be sorted. All
they needed was to be together again.

The following thirty-six hours were among the longest
she had ever known. She spent the whole of Wednesday

polishing up the article, and most of the night restless. The morning rush hour left her drained of what little energy she had managed to accumulate.

'You look like someone who's been burning the candle at both ends,' commented Ben the moment she showed her face round his office door. 'I sent you out there to look at life, not live it!'

'I'm still suffering from an eight-hour time-lag,' she defended. 'Plus twelve at least thumping a typewriter.' She placed the buff envelope file down on the desk in front of him. 'There it is. Hope you like it.'

'So do I.' He studied her shrewdly. 'Any idea when Wilde's planning on bringing his stuff in?'

'He didn't say,' she acknowledged.

'How'd you two get on anyway?' he asked. 'You didn't seem to be hitting it off so well at the outset.'

Alex kept her expression strictly neutral. 'We managed. He was right about one thing: a fortnight's nowhere near long enough to get to grips with a country like Japan. The people are so... different.'

'Obviously they're different,' Ben returned drily. 'They're Japanese. If that's the sum total of what you've come up with, you'll be out of a job come going-home time!'

'Read it and see,' she invited. 'I write better than I talk.'

'You'd have to.' He waved a dismissive hand as the telephone rang. 'See you later.'

Tony Jackman dropped by her desk half-way through the morning. 'Thought you'd decided to stay over there permanently,' he remarked. 'Enjoy it, did you?'

Alex donned a bland expression, too well aware of the professional resentment behind the seemingly casual tone. 'Very much, thanks. It's a great place.'

'Be interesting to see how far under the surface you got.' His tone altered subtly. 'Rumour has it you and Wilde are old acquaintances. That must have made things easier.'

'Much,' she agreed, not about to be drawn. 'Into anything interesting yourself at the moment?' she tagged on.

He shrugged. 'Depends what you call interesting. Some anthropologist has come up with another of those lost tribes in New Guinea. Ben's considering sending along a team.'

Alex cocked a questioning glance. 'You're not too keen on the idea?'

'Would you be?'

She sidestepped the question. 'Ben isn't likely to look too kindly on a refusal.'

'He didn't offer *me* the job yet.' He lifted a laconic hand. 'See you.'

Which meant there was a possibility Ben was waiting to see what kind of a job she had made of this assignment, Alex reflected. If she and Greg were not to further their relationship after all, then the New Guinea expedition would be just the thing she needed to take her mind off it. Otherwise . . . well, that would be something to consider if and when.

She was the first to arrive at the restaurant, growing steadily more morose over a drink for fifteen minutes before Greg finally put in an appearance.

'Sorry,' he said, sliding into his seat. 'It's been one of those mornings.' Blue eyes appraised her, expression as unreadable as always. 'You look tired,' was the summing up.

If one more person told her that, thought Alex, she would scream! She *was* tired. Not just physically, but all the way through. 'I'll survive,' she said. 'Did you develop the films yet?'

'Of course.' He was sitting back in the chair, fingers toying with the stem of the wineglass in front of him. 'I'm taking them in this afternoon.'

'Are you happy with them?'

His mouth tilted with faint sardonicism. 'I try to give good value. How about your stuff?'

'Ben didn't pronounce yet.' She made her tone matter-of-fact. 'That could mean he's been too busy to take a look at it—or that he's gearing himself up to tell me it's no good.'

'From what I know of Ben Reynolds, he wouldn't waste any time. If he'd had any doubts about your ability he wouldn't have offered you the job in the first place.' His glance went over her again, his tone altering. 'You did lose some weight this last couple of weeks. Maybe you should see a doctor.'

Head or heart? she wondered with fleeting cynicism. She looked back at him silently for a moment, attempting to come to terms with the whole situation. For two weeks she had lived in close confines with this man— had made love with unbridled passion. It was enough for her to know how she felt, but was it enough for him? Even now she had no real idea of what he might be thinking.

'I think,' he said levelly and unexpectedly, almost as if in answer to an unspoken question, 'that we should get married as soon as possible. That is, unless you've changed your mind again?'

The emotions flooding her were too complex to be separated out. It was with a sense of surprise that she heard herself saying quite calmly, 'How soon are we talking about?'

He smiled, lifting his shoulders. 'How about my birthday? That way I'm not likely to forget the anniversary.'

The temptation to fling all caution aside was great. Alex resisted it with an effort. 'Why the sudden rush?' she asked unsteadily.

'Because I think we both need the security,' he said. He smiled again. 'Plus I'm not sure I can take the strain of a regular courtship!' The smile faded, replaced by an urgency that stirred her every sense. 'Alex, I've spent the last forty-eight hours thinking this through. We have everything going for us.'

Everything except the one thing she needed to hear above all else, she thought. All the same, she was going to say yes, because to say no and mean it was totally beyond her. She loved him so much, it was an actual pain inside her.

'That only gives us just over a fortnight,' she said on a husky note. 'It's going to cause a lot of talk.'

'Does that matter?' He reached for her hand, eyes very blue in the tan of his face. 'We're going to do this whole thing by the book, so first stop after we've finished here is a jewellers to find you a ring.'

'You sound as if you had it all planned,' she said, tremoring to the warmth and hard strength of his fingers. 'Were you so sure of me, Greg?'

'I was sure of what I wanted,' he declared. 'I could only hope you felt the same way after two days on your own.'

Her own eyes widened a little. 'You mean you left me purposely?'

'That's right. You weren't all that sure of anything any more when we got our feet back on home soil again. I had to give you the opportunity to think things over.'

The waiter was approaching to take their order, and they hadn't even glanced at the menu yet. Heart suddenly lighter than it had been in ages, she said, 'I'll have whatever you're having.'

The grin was reminiscent of old times. 'All the way through,' he said.

They called in at Garrards on the way back to the office. Trying on rings from the selection presented by the well-mannered young salesman, Alex felt as if she were in a dream. Only a few hours ago she had been so miserably sure that it was all over between her and Greg again, and now here they were actually getting engaged! In the end, it was Greg himself who picked out the diamond cluster, sliding it on to her finger with a gesture in no way restricted by the salesman's smiling observation.

'That's the one,' he stated.

Alex could find no fault with the choice. That Greg expected her to wear it as of now was made obvious when he picked up the box taken from an inner drawer and pocketed it before taking out his cheque book. They were in the car again before she could bring herself to say anything.

'It must have cost a fortune!' she got out.

His laugh was genuine. 'A small one, maybe. The fee I'm getting from *World* will help.'

'I thought that was going towards the rates,' she said.

'Is that what I told you?' He sounded amused. 'I must have been looking for sympathy.' He glanced her way briefly, the smile still playing around his lips. 'You're not marrying a pauper.'

Something inside her relaxed. She smiled back, for the first time allowing herself to believe that they were doing the right thing. 'I'm glad to hear it!'

'I know your parents are dead,' he said after a moment or two, 'but do you have any other family left?'

'A couple of aunts in Bristol,' she acknowledged. 'They haven't shown a lot of interest in what I've been doing with myself these last few years, I don't imagine my getting married is going to rouse any sudden display.'

'They might surprise you. Anyway, my folks will make up for any lack—my mother especially. She was beginning to despair of ever becoming a grandmother!'

Alex slid a glance sideways at the long-fingered hands on the wheel, trying to visualise them as chubby baby ones. For the first time she found herself wondering what he had been like as a child. Independent, no doubt. Any child of theirs would inherit characteristics from both sides—an amalgam, hopefully, of the better points. The thought of having Greg's child made her feel suddenly soft and warm inside. She was going broody already, she thought, trying to laugh it off, but the feeling persisted. It was what he wanted; he had said so. And it would certainly help cement their marriage.

She was getting too far ahead, she reflected at that point. At least get the honeymoon over with first!

'Where would you like to go?' he asked, apparently reading her mind again. 'I'm open to suggestion.'

'I don't suppose you'd fancy a trip to New Guinea?' she murmured, waiting for a reaction that failed to materialise.

'Is that your next assignment?'

'I'm not sure,' she admitted. 'It could be possible.' She paused before tagging on diffidently, 'Would you object?'

'Why should I?' He sounded quite calm about it. 'It's your job. We make a good team. Maybe it's worth thinking about at that. Depends on Reynolds. He does have staff photographers.'

'Not in your class,' she interjected. 'He'd leap at the chance to use you again!'

'Let's wait and see,' he responded drily. 'I don't come all that cheap.'

'Are you going to tell your parents I'm the same girl you were living with two years ago?' she asked as they slowed for the lights. 'Assuming they knew about it, of course.'

'I might have mentioned it in letters,' he said easily enough. 'There's no point trying to hide it. Mother will have a full case history out of you inside the first twenty-four hours. You can always get round the reason we parted by saying we had a misunderstanding. The very idea of our getting together again will satisfy her romantic streak.' They were in sight of the *World* offices. He added, 'You'd better hop out here while I go and find a parking spot.'

'If you'd use taxis instead of dragging this around you wouldn't have to bother,' she returned, preparing to leave the car as he drew up outside the building. 'You could be looking for hours!'

The smile he gave her was long and slow. 'All part of the challenge. See you upstairs.'

Ben's secretary phoned through not two minutes after Alex reached her desk. She responded tentatively to the summons, her confidence evaporating by the second. The buff file was at the editor's elbow when she went into the office. In that first moment, as he looked up at her, she was certain he was going to say her efforts were a waste of time and money. When he did speak, the relief and pleasure were overwhelming.

'You've done a good job,' he said. 'Better even than I anticipated. If the photography matches up we're going to have a great feature!'

Praise of such magnitude from Ben Reynolds was almost unheard of. Alex could feel her ego swelling as she stood. 'Greg will be here in a moment,' she said, attempting to dampen it down a little. 'He's parking the car.' She hesitated, knowing it had to come out some time but still reluctant to have anyone else in on the fact. 'It's probably going to come as a big surprise,' she began, then paused and thrust out her left hand. 'Greg and I are engaged.'

'Seems I wasn't too far wrong about you two, after all,' said Ben with irony. 'Though why you made out you were strangers beats me. When's the wedding to be?'

Her mind balked at that. 'Soon,' she compromised.

'Not too soon, I hope. I may have another job lined up for you.'

Alex smiled. 'New Guinea, by any chance?'

'Could be.' He lifted an eyebrow. 'Interested?'

'Would I be anything else?' She paused before adding levelly, 'Might *you* be interested in sending the same team along?'

The eyebrow rose even further. 'You mean he'd be willing?'

'He might.' She was suddenly cautious, not wholly sure Greg hadn't been joking. Her laugh was meant to signify as much. 'We might even make it a honeymoon!'

'What some men will do for love!' Ben was neither put out nor off. 'It's an idea worth considering—depending on what he's done with the Japanese end, of course.'

Greg's arrival forestalled any comment. Alex turned her head with a slightly fixed smile, still too much a stranger to the situation to feel totally at ease. 'That was quick.'

'I took a chance,' he acknowledged. His gaze rested on her face. 'I gather the verdict was good?'

It was Ben himself who answered. 'Good enough. I understand congratulations are in order.'

Blue eyes found green again for a moment, the former holding an odd expression. 'Thanks.' He moved forward past Alex to lay his briefcase on the desk and extract a large brown envelope. 'I've picked out a few dozen prints to give you a good choice of subject matter. We can either go through them now or I can leave them with you.'

Ben was already opening the envelope, waving a hand towards the chair beside Alex. 'No time like the present.'

There was a lengthy pause while he leafed through the pile of prints. Alex slid her eyes in Greg's direction, but he was gazing out through the window, face averted. The crisp line of the dark hair across the back of his neck brought an aching hunger. They were going to be together tonight, she hoped—or at least for part of it. Whether at her place or his didn't matter all that much, although *he* didn't have to pull out the bed before getting into it. Everything would be all right once she was in his arms again. It was the only place she wanted to be right now.

'It's going to be a difficult choice,' Ben decreed, completing his initial perusal. 'They all tie in well with the text. We'll work up a rough layout before making any final decisions.' He picked up one of the prints to study it afresh. 'I always thought *geishas* were glorified pros. Some of these look little more than children!'

'Things aren't always what they seem.' Greg was moving as he spoke, heaving himself to his feet. 'Glad you like them.'

The editor laughed. 'You could say it was a worthwhile trip in all directions! One or two minor details I'd like to go over, Alex,' he added as she made to accompany Greg from the office. 'When you're through.'

'I've an appointment at half past, anyway,' said Greg from the doorway as she hesitated. 'I should be back at the studio by six.'

'I'll see you there, then,' Alex agreed.

It was gone five before she finally got away. She was able to grab a taxi cruising past, settling back into her seat to view the coming evening with a mixture of anticipation and uncertainty. If Greg had been serious about getting married on his birthday, arrangements were going to have to be made fairly sharpish. People were going to speculate about the haste, but that was by the way. They would find out soon enough that she wasn't pregnant. The New Guinea trip wouldn't be until the end of September. Ben wanted an answer within the week—to include Greg too if he were willing to take it on. She still wasn't sure about that.

She had the taxi drop her across the road from the studio due to the difficulty in turning across the thronging traffic. As it was, she had to take her life in her hands in order to make it on foot. The pretty young blonde girl behind the reception desk looked up on her entry, switching on a smile.

'You must be Alex,' she said. 'I'm Mandy. Greg phoned a few minutes ago to say he'd be a bit late.' She came over to slide the bolts on the outer door, adding over a shoulder, 'They're all out on jobs, so there's no point in my hanging around any longer. The percolator's on upstairs if you feel like some coffee while you're waiting.'

'Why don't you have some with me?' invited Alex on impulse. 'Unless you're in a hurry to get home, of course?'

The smile came again, accompanied by a regretful shake of the head. 'I'd have loved to, but I'm meeting someone in half an hour. I suppose you'll be round here often enough now. Congratulations, by the way.'

'Thanks.' Alex could think of nothing more riveting to say. Greg had lost no time in spreading the word, it seemed.

Double-glazing kept the flat free of all but a minor hum from the traffic outside. Alex poured herself a cup of excellent coffee in the kitchen, and took it through with her to the sitting-room. It seemed an age since she had last been here, she mused, taking a seat on one of the chesterfields. So much had happened since then— so much was still to happen. In another two weeks she would be living here on a permanent basis as Greg's wife—a thought that brought a warming glow. It was going to be a good marriage because they would both be working at it. Perhaps lacking a little in some respects, but one couldn't have everything.

Oh, God, she thought in sudden desperation, make him love me!

There was a portfolio on the table in front of her. Putting down her cup, she flipped it open, leafing idly through the prints it contained. Casual shots, most of them, she realised. Here was the one he had taken of her that first morning, leaning over the bridge rail in the *ryoken* garden, and another of her poised to dive from the side of Tsugi's boat. The villagers of Usukimiya would shortly be about their daily business, she reflected. It would be a sad day when the pearl fishing had to end, but that was the price of progress. Cultured pearls, perfectly matched in size and shape and colour, were the big profit-makers these days. In how many places right here in England had the old crafts been buried by the more profitable economics of mass production? It might be interesting to delve deeper into that subject.

A sudden lump came into her throat as she looked at the print she had just revealed. Yuki was wearing the dragon kimono in which she had greeted them at her parents' home, her hands hidden within the wide sleeves in time-honoured fashion, her eyes so enigmatic in their slanting gaze. She didn't recall his taking the photograph, so it must have been when she was elsewhere— when the two of them were alone together. He didn't keep Japanese memorabilia around the place, he had said, but this was different, wasn't it? This was perhaps his only memento of the woman he loved beyond all.

The sound of a car drawing up in the courtyard below jerked her out of it. Closing the portfolio, she composed herself for Greg's entry. She could hardly object to his keeping the photograph; she had no intention of even mentioning it. By the time he saw Yuki again—if ever— he was going to be a husband, perhaps even a father. If children would help keep them together, she would give him half a dozen!

He came in via the rear premises, his smile when he saw her sitting there a reassurance in itself.

'Sorry again,' he said. 'Obviously you got my message, or you wouldn't be here.'

'Mandy waited to let me in,' Alex confirmed. 'I'm surprised you don't put *her* in front of the camera. She's really lovely!'

'I already did,' he said. 'Oddly enough, she isn't very photogenic. I spent an hour or more lighting her and still wasn't happy with the results. She's better off sticking with her original ambition.'

'A rich old man? Not much to hope for, is it?'

'Depends on the viewpoint.' He moved across to the drinks' tray to pour himself a whisky, adding lightly, 'Not my type, if that's what you're getting round to asking.'

'It hadn't crossed my mind,' she said truthfully. 'You always used to say you found blondes too chocolate-boxy.' Catching his sideways glance, she sighed and shook her head. 'Which gave me even less foundation for suspecting you of having an affair with Samantha Price, I suppose.'

'Reason didn't come into it, did it?' His shrug dismissed the subject as of no present importance. 'Where would you like to eat?'

'Here,' she said. 'I saw a couple of steaks in the fridge.'

'That's what I hoped you'd say.' He cocked an eyebrow. 'Fancy cooking some while I have a well-earned shower and shave?'

Her answering smile held mock resignation. 'I suppose I have to familiarise myself with your kitchen some time.'

'A girl after my own heart,' he stated with an irony that could have been unintentional. He downed the rest of the whisky before making for the door. 'Fifteen minutes.'

Alex grilled the steaks and made a salad bowl with a rice and mushroom accompaniment. The kitchen cupboards were well stocked, she noted. Obviously he didn't eat out all the time. Having so much space to work in made all the difference, she conceded, thinking of her own tiny area. Not that she intended spending all her time in the kitchen, by any means. There was more to life than cooking!

Greg was wearing trousers and shirt when he came through. 'You should have brought your *yukata*,' he said as he took his place at the table. 'This looks good! But then,' he added, 'you could turn your hand to most things.'

'Such flattery,' she responded, borrowing his mood, 'deserves a reward. I opened a bottle of your Aloxe-Corton, by the way.'

'So I see. By rights, it should be champagne.' He was watching her as he said it, registering the faint jerk of her head. 'After all, we do have something to celebrate.'

'Did you really mean it when you said you might consider the New Guinea trip' she asked hesitantly. 'Or were you just having a joke?'

'I never joke about work,' he denied. 'I take it you've been offered the job?'

'So have you, if you're willing. Ben jumped at the idea.'

'Did he now?' There was no telling anything from his tone. 'When is it to be?'

'The end of September. A whole month away yet. We'll be going in by helicopter to within half a day's march of the tribe, so that's going to save a lot of time. We shouldn't be away longer than a week all told.'

'I'll have to check my schedule,' he said, 'but I'm interested all right. Let's eat before the steaks go cold.'

They took coffee over by the fire Greg had turned on against the unseasonal coolness of the evening. Sitting there in the glow, Alex felt almost content. Greg was lounging comfortably in a deep easy chair, one ankle resting across the other knee. Sometimes in the past they had sat like this by lamplight just talking, she remembered. If he had been thinking of Yuki Nagasowa then it hadn't been obvious—any more than it was now. Few people loved only the once. No doubt there would eventually have been someone else for her if she hadn't met Greg again. Not quite the same, of course, but not necessarily any less meaningful either.

'You've gone pensive again,' he said softly.

'I was thinking about what I should wear for the wedding,' she claimed without haste.

He laughed. 'The perennial cry, I suppose—I haven't a single thing in my wardrobe!'

'The "something new" is usually the outfit,' Alex rejoined equably.

'In which case, I'd better try talking my tailor into a quick fit.' He straightened to put down the coffee-cup, holding out a hand to her. 'Come on over here.'

There was no hesitation in accepting the invitation. She had been waiting for it too long. Putting her hand in his, she allowed herself to be drawn into his arms.

'It's going to work out fine,' he said with emphasis. 'Believe me, Alex.'

With his mouth on hers and the familiar tumult springing inside her, she could believe anything. They made love right there on the floor in front of the mock coals. One day, Alex promised herself when her head had stopped spinning, they might manage a real fire. A house in the country, perhaps, with a real garden and trees—like the one her grandparents had lived in. Theirs had been a lasting marriage. They had even died within a few months of each other.

It was Greg who made the first move, sitting up decisively. 'Waiting till after we're married to move in with me is ridiculous! It's still early enough. We can collect your immediate needs and do the rest at the weekend.'

Alex gazed up at the firm profile, feeling her heart-beats quicken again. 'You said it was putting the cart before the horse,' she murmured.

'I've said a whole lot of things that don't have any bearing right now,' he admitted. His mouth relaxed as he looked at her, voice taking on a softer note. 'I've missed you these last two nights. Another fortnight would drive me up the wall!'

She would have preferred some other, less physical need, but it was too soon to expect it. She said slowly, 'I'm supposed to give a month's notice.'

'Your rent's paid in advance,' he pointed out. 'I doubt if anyone is going to complain if you move out ahead of time—especially if they can re-let it right away.' He leaned down to kiss her again, cherishing her mouth until her blood sang in her ears. 'What do you say?'

Her own voice sounded rough. 'I can do some sorting out while I'm about it—get rid of all the stuff I've been meaning to throw out for ages. Luckily the furniture came with the flat.'

His smile held triumph but no mockery. 'No need to be too ruthless. There's plenty of cupboard-space going begging.' He pressed himself to his feet, holding out a hand to draw her to hers. 'No time like the present, as Ben would say. We can be back in a couple of hours.'

The drive out to Wimbledon was accomplished in record time. Deciding what to take and what to leave for the time being took longer than Alex had anticipated. In the end it was Greg himself who said enough was enough, closing up the two suitcases and hoisting them out to the car while she scribbled a note for the milkman who delivered her daily pint.

'I'll phone the agency in the morning,' she said when they were on their way back to town. 'I can drop the keys in after we clear the rest out at the weekend.'

'By which time they'll most likely have another client already lined up for it,' Greg commented drily.

And her boats would be well and truly burned, came the thought. Well, they'd be that anyway in a couple of weeks' time.

The walk-in wardrobe at Greg's flat was more than adequate for two. Greg made more coffee while she hung away her things, and brought it through to the bedroom. She could see him through the dressing-table mirror as she laid out her cosmetic tray, back comfortably propped by pillows. He was leafing through an old copy of *World* she had brought with her, pausing to skim an article here and there. A lock of the dark hair had fallen forward over his forehead the way it always did if not brushed back into place. Even in repose, his features retained their vitality of line.

He looked up suddenly and caught her eye through the mirror, his smile slow and heart-jerking. 'Quite like old times, isn't it?' he said. 'Why don't you leave that and come on over here?'

She went because she couldn't help herself to sit down on the mattress edge and feel his arms close about her. His mouth was tender, the long, clever fingers caressing her back through the thin cotton of her blouse. The faint, elusive scent of him tantalised her nostrils.

'What made you change?' she asked softly between kisses. 'The aftershave, I mean. You always wore Lauder before.'

'It doesn't do to become too set in one's ways,' he said. 'I changed a whole lot of things after you left.' His fingers traced the line of her jaw to find the sensitive area behind her ear, shortening her breath as they delicately explored. Blue eyes assessed her response with a smile. 'There's no rush,' he murmured. 'We have all night. Just like it used to be.'

Not quite, thought Alex mistily. She was older, wiser, aware that few things were perfect. The main thing was that the two of them were together again, and this time it was going to stay that way.

Life settled into a pattern of sorts over the following days. She couldn't, Alex told herself often, be happier. Both Greg's two assistants and Mandy had accepted her presence as a matter of course. It was only in her own mind that any awkwardness lingered.

Saturday came round again, bringing with it the necessity of finalising arrangements for both wedding and reception, the latter of which was to be held in a private suite at the Ritz. Greg's parents were due to arrive in London on the Thursday. Alex had already spoken with his mother on the telephone, a conversation that had left her free from at least one source of concern. Sylvia Wilde had been obviously and openly delighted at the news. She had, she said, begun to believe her son was destined to stay a bachelor all his life!

With Greg out on an early job, and no office to go to, there was time for a leisurely breakfast for once. Mandy gave her a welcoming smile when she went down later to see if there was any personal post.

'There's a letter for Greg,' she said, picking up an airmail envelope. 'He'd gone before it arrived.'

Alex took it from her, steeling herself to show no reaction as she looked at the Japanese stamp. It was addressed in English—well, it would have to be, wouldn't it?—the writing small and neat. She could visualise

Yuki's smooth and lovely face, the gleaming coil of black hair. All the hard-won confidence had flown, ousted by a dull depression like a weight pressing down on her head.

She left the letter where Greg was bound to see it if he returned before she did. Never had a morning seemed so long, the people she spoke with so obtuse. Whatever detail was still to be taken care of could wait, she decided at one o'clock. She had to find out why Yuki had written so soon after a leavetaking that had seemed so final at the time.

Greg was in ahead of her. Alex tried to stop her eyes from straying in search of the blue envelope as she answered his greeting.

'I've already eaten,' he acknowledged when she asked. 'I'd have waited for you if I'd known you were going to be back this early. Run into any problems?'

Alex shook her head, not trusting her voice. There was nothing in his manner to suggest any underlying emotion, yet he had to be feeling *some*thing.

If he noted her constraint he made no comment. 'I'm going down to have a word with Colin before he leaves,' he said. He was almost at the door before he added over a shoulder, 'There was a letter from Yuki. Read it if you want to. It's on the TV cabinet.'

'I can't read Japanese,' she said.

'You don't have to. She writes English better than I read Japanese. You'll have no difficulty understanding it.'

Left alone, Alex forced herself to walk over and pick up the envelope, to extract the two thin sheets of paper covered in the same copperplate script. Yuki opened with the polite platitudes so beloved of her race, enquiring after the health and well-being of both Greg himself and that of his parents. From the cautious manner in which her own name was mentioned, it was immediately apparent that news of their impending marriage had not yet reached the writer, who went on to speak of other matters. Only in the final paragraph did the whole tone of the letter alter, the words leaping from the page with sickening impact.

> I have decided, after all these years, that love of a man transcends duty. Only you can make my parents understand our emotions, Greg. It is my hope and trust that you will try. When you read this I shall already be gone from Tokyo. We have wasted so much time, dear friend, and life is so short.

With fingers that felt all thumbs, Alex carefully folded the letter back into its original creases and returned it to the envelope. The dull pain under her ribs was spreading, reaching out to every part of her body. Yuki was on her way here to England—perhaps already in the country—to find the man she loved before it was too late. Not Greg's fault. He had obviously given up hope of ever changing her mind. He had left her here alone to read the letter because he couldn't find a better way of telling her it was all over between them.

So what now? she wondered numbly. She would have to find a new flat for a start. The thought of being on her own again was soul-destroying. Better if she had never said yes at all than to face this kind of pain.

She was standing at the window looking out on to the busy scene below when Greg returned to the room.

'Incidentally,' he said, 'I booked a table at Lacy's for eight o'clock. No other plans, have you?' There was a silence when she failed to reply. She could feel his eyes boring into her unresponsive back. When he spoke again it was on a different note. 'Alex? What is it?'

Her laugh had a bitter edge. 'You can ask me that after giving me Yuki's letter to read?'

He was behind her before she knew he had moved, taking her by the shoulders to turn her to face him. He looked genuinely perplexed, she thought detachedly. Strange he should bother to put on any act.

'What are you talking about?' he demanded.

'You don't have to pretend,' she said. 'I know how you must be feeling. Only don't ask me to have any sympathy for her too, because I can't. She should have made up her mind before this—a long time before this!'

The blue eyes had acquired a glazed look. 'Let me get this straight,' he said slowly. 'You think Yuki is coming *here*—to *me*?'

Alex stared at him in sudden confusion. 'Isn't that what she says?'

'No, it isn't. Right now she's in Nagasaki with the man she's going to marry at last.'

She said blankly. 'But she told me...'

'Told you what?' Greg prompted as her voice tailed away.

'That the man she loved was forbidden to her,' she said in dawning realisation. 'I thought she meant you!'

His smile was faint. 'The family of the man she loves have been sworn enemies of the Nagasowas for more than a hundred years. These things aren't easily put aside in Japan even today. I'm glad she's seen sense in the end. Haruo will come round to it eventually.'

'Will you?' she asked low-toned, and saw his brows draw together again.

'Why shouldn't I? I've been trying to persuade her for years.'

'Even though you loved her yourself?'

The lean features took on a new expression. 'I've told you before, there's love and love. What I feel for her doesn't have any bearing on what I feel for you.'

She said heavily, 'I know that. You've made it plain enough. I satisfy your body, she appeals to your sensibilities.'

He was looking at her oddly, almost uncertainly. 'Alex, what exactly do *you* feel?' he asked.

The time for prevarication was long past. She looked back at him without flinching. 'I love you. I never stopped loving you, Greg. I just lost sight of what love really meant.'

A muscle jerked suddenly in the clean jawline. Next moment he was holding her close with his face against her hair. 'I've been waiting for you to give me some sign,' he murmured thickly. 'I laid myself open two years ago and got kicked in the groin. This time I had to be sure of you.' He bent to slide an arm under her knees, swinging her up and carrying her across to the nearest sofa. 'I love you,' said fiercely between kisses. '*Only* you—this way. If I'd realised . . .' He broke off, straightening to look at her with apology in his eyes. 'I've been out to save face since the minute we met again. One glance and I was up to my neck in it. If it's any consolation, I've been through hell this last few weeks. Finding out what I did about our break-up nearly finished me.'

'I'm sorry,' she got out, but he put a finger to her lips.

'I know that—now. What I couldn't do was accept it right away. I wanted to hurt you. It took that time when you nearly drowned to fetch me up short. Even then, I resented the way I felt about you.'

'What changed your mind?' Alex whispered.

'You did.' He smoothed the back of his hand down her cheek, his eyes warm and tender, the way they used to be in the past before she had robbed him of his masculine pride with that letter. 'I finally realised there was no way I was ever going to get you out of my blood. Marriage seemed the only way of holding on to you in the end. I'd have fought tooth and nail to preserve it, whether you learned to love me or not.'

'What about Yuki?' she forced herself to ask.

He smiled a little. 'She's like a sister to me.'

'Was she always?'

'No,' he admitted. 'There was a time when I imagined I wanted to marry her. She was the one who set me straight—made me see how it could never work, even if she'd returned the feeling. Then I met you, and I knew she was right. What I felt for her didn't even come close to the real thing.'

'And I ruined it all,' she said softly. 'Oh, Greg, I was so dense! We could have had all that time together. Two whole years!'

'They're behind us now,' he said. 'We're lucky we got another chance. And this time we're not going to let anything break us up. If it needs saying we air it. Right?'

'Right.' Alex slid her arms about his neck to bring him close against her, thrilling as always to the feel of his lean hard body. 'I want you, Greg.' There was urgency in the plea. 'I want you now!'

His smile was slow, the fire already smouldering. 'That's what I like, a woman who knows her own mind!'

It had been good between them before, Alex thought mistily as he kissed her, but never quite like this! It was going to be a long and loving marriage, with no more misunderstandings and nasty suspicions. They were starting anew

Harlequin Presents.

Coming Next Month

Available in October wherever paperback books are sold, or through Harlequin Reader Service:

In the U.S.
901 Fuhrmann Blvd.
P.O. Box 1397
Buffalo, N.Y. 14240-1397

In Canada
P.O. Box 603
Fort Erie, Ontario
L2A 5X3

Have You Ever Wondered If You Could Write A Harlequin Novel?

Here's great news—Harlequin is offering a series of cassette tapes to help you do just that. Written by Harlequin editors, these tapes give practical advice on how to make your characters—and your story—come alive. There's a tape for each contemporary romance series Harlequin publishes.

Mail order only

All sales final

TO: *Harlequin Reader Service*
Audiocassette Tape Offer
P.O. Box 1396
Buffalo, NY 14269-1396

I enclose a check/money order payable to HARLEQUIN READER SERVICE® for $9.70 ($8.95 plus 75¢ postage and handling) for EACH tape ordered for the total sum of $_____*
Please send:

☐ Romance and Presents   ☐ Intrigue
☐ American Romance   ☐ Temptation
☐ Superromance   ☐ All five tapes ($38.80 total)

Signature_____
                                                (please print clearly)
Name:_____

Address:_____

State:_____ Zip:_____

*Iowa and New York residents add appropriate sales tax   AUDIO-H

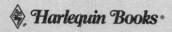
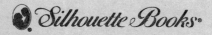